THIS
LOVE

By Deanna Roy

USA Today bestselling author of

Forever Innocent ~ Forever Loved
Forever Sheltered ~ Forever Bound
Forever Family ~ Forever Christmas
Stella and Dane

Forbidden Dance ~ Wounded Dance
Wicked Dance ~ Tender Dance
Final Dance ~ Billionaire's Dance

Never miss a new release.
Sign up for emails or texts at www.deannaroy.com/news

THIS LOVE

By Deanna Roy

Casey Shay Press
PO Box 160116
Austin, TX 78716
www.caseyshaypress.com

Paperback Edition ISBN: 9781938150746

The heart remembers.

For Elizabeth
and all the epilepsy warriors.

Go forth and keep fighting.

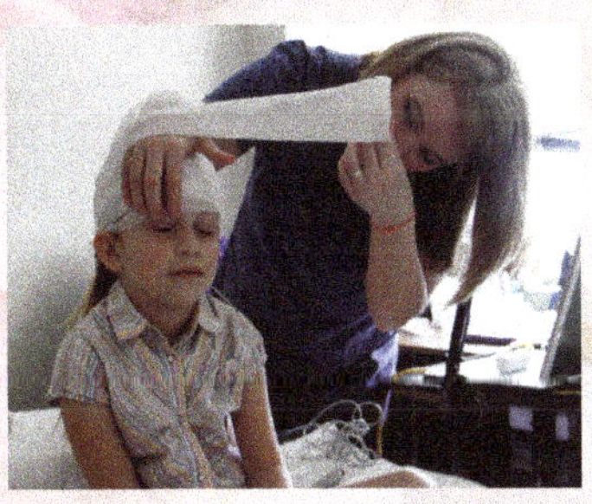

Purple day is March 26.
Wear purple and post instructions from epilepsy.com
to raise awareness on how to help someone
who might have a seizure in front of you.

That person could be my daughter.

The heart remembers.

The heart remembers.

CHAPTER 1

Tucker

My mom, back when she was alive, loved poetry.

I never really understood it, being a twelve-year-old numbskull who'd rather be zapping zombies on my PlayStation.

She'd quote one of them all the time. Something like, "She walks in beauty."

It had a line about a cheek and a smile.

I could probably Google it, but at that moment, with the first glow of morning casting across Ava's face, I didn't need the words.

I had the feeling.

Rosy. Content. She *sleeps* in beauty.

Ha. *Sleeping beauty.* Suddenly, the fairy tale made sense, too. I'd cut down thorn bushes to get to her. Could I defeat a dragon?

Maybe those PlayStation hours I'd logged as a kid would come in handy if I had to wield a sword and aim for an imaginary jugular.

But this morning seemed the right kind for poems.

This afternoon, Ava and I would get married.

It felt like a long time coming, but we had met young when we were only seventeen. In the eight years since then, I'd found her, lost her, and found her again, like a river traversing a mountainside.

I hoped the wedding would be a linchpin, a moment in time we could look back on as, yes, this was the day we committed to this course, no matter where it took us.

Ava slept soundly and hated how alarms startled her like a shock to the heart. I leaned over to stroke her pale cheek with the back of my fingers to rouse her gently.

Another line returned from that long-latent memory.

"Mellowed to that tender light."

I glanced at the ceiling, as if Mom might be there, feeding me the words. "Thanks for being here," I whispered. Thirteen years gone, along with my father and younger brother, lost in an instant, leaving only me to survive the crash.

But today, on this day, she was with me.

Ava shifted toward me. "What did you say? I missed it."

"Just good morning." I leaned over to kiss her cheek. "Happy wedding day."

She smiled. "But this is the one day you don't have to get up early."

My hours at Jiffy Lube normally started at seven. Ava worked for herself and never stirred before nine.

"But it's the one day you do." I stayed close, reveling in the sleepy warmth of her neck and bare shoulder.

She blew out a gust of air. "Right. Hairdresser. Makeup artist." She rolled into me, tucking her head against my chest. "How about I sleep in and rely on my natural beauty?"

"Works for me." I pulled her in more tightly.

She lay there for a few more seconds, then blew out another huff. "I can't. Tina would be disappointed. So would Dad."

"And your sisters." Ava's father had a second family who adored her. "They're all so excited to do girly things with you."

Ava kicked the covers aside. "I regret agreeing to this big production. We should have eloped."

"Not too late. I can sneak you out of the house."

But at that moment, a car door slammed. Then another. Cheerful voices filtered up from the yard.

Then the front door opened. Ava's stepmother Tina had a spare key. All our close friends and family did. They worried about us. They had their reasons.

Ava ducked beneath the sheets, visible only as a spray of long, brown hair fanned over the pillow.

I burrowed my way next to her until I could make out her shadowy face. "You think they'll find us in here?"

Fingernails tapped on the bedroom door. "Ava? You up? It's time."

Ava's face tilted toward mine. "That's Tina."

"I think you're stuck."

"Okay." She leaned forward to kiss me lightly on the mouth, then threw the sheets down. "Coming!" she called.

I pulled on her arm to drag her in for another kiss before I let her go. "See you this afternoon," I said. "I'll be the one in the black tux."

"I'll be all in white," she said. "Unless I make a run for it."

"You'd better take me with you."

She grinned. "Of course." Then she was up, opening the door in her tank top and shorts, slipping into the hall.

I stayed in her warm spot a moment longer, trying to

remember more of the poem. It felt like a gift. I had a feeling Mom knew I'd miss her, miss all of them, on a day like this.

I picked up my phone and Googled the words I remembered. The full text showed up easily. Lord Byron.

"She walks in beauty, like the night / Of cloudless climes and starry skies."

It fit. Mom couldn't have predicted who I would meet years after she was gone. But all those words suited Ava. Night. Cloudless. Starry.

Gram had been with me that day eight years ago when Ava turned up at the children's hospital, wired for seizures, same as me. We were about to age out of pediatrics.

Epilepsy had been a battle for both of us, but now, in our mid-twenties, it felt like we had it licked. With puberty and growth spurts and hormonal imbalances behind us, we had treatments that worked. Meds for her. An implanted device for me.

Life was good. And with hope came optimism, so we made the leap to marriage, even though I was taking college classes while working full time.

Her photography business was thriving. She had even hired an assistant, Vinnie, who would photograph our wedding today.

Normal life finally seemed possible.

I slid out of the covers and headed to the window. Down below, Tina's car gleamed on the curb. It looked out of place against the line of weary houses in need of paint, like a shiny diamond in the dirt.

It wasn't a fancy neighborhood like theirs in Houston. But Ava and I were making our own way. We were proud of what we'd accomplished, despite everything life had thrown at us.

I turned to the closet. Time for me to head to Gram's house to meet up with my best buds, Bill and Fuentes. We had it easy with nothing more to do than getting dressed in our fancy duds and driving over to the country club in the late afternoon.

It would be a good day.

And Mom, sitting on whatever star looked down on us, had somehow made sure it started out exactly right.

Maybe I'd add a little Lord Byron to my vows.

CHAPTER 2

Ava

I spent the morning getting my hair tugged, my face painted, and my nails sparkled up.

Each woman who assisted during the day had her own philosophy about weddings.

The hairdresser, who brushed out the curls only to pin them up again, which struck me as terribly pointless, told me, "This is the day you two will love each other the least."

I puzzled over this one for a while before Tina leaned in to say, "I think she means you will love each other more and more every day after this."

That hadn't been the case for my parents. My mother ran my father off, then lied about him for nearly a decade. I only learned how he really felt when I escaped her.

She wasn't invited to the wedding.

But I didn't say this to the hairdresser.

Not to the nail tech either, when she told me, "This is the happiest day of your life."

I couldn't see how anyone would think that. So far, it

had been frustrating and nerve-racking and scheduled to the nines.

A much happier day for me was spent photographing Lady Bird Lake in the center of Austin, the sunlight dancing over the waves. I'd point out to Tucker that the reflections looked like the water had shiny braces, and he would laugh and tell me how much he loved how I described the world.

Maybe I'd understand what the nail tech meant when I got to the end of the day. It could be that the moment we stood in front of the Justice of the Peace and said our vows that all the pain of preparation would evaporate. People said that about childbirth, too.

I wasn't buying it. Not yet anyway.

The makeup artist came last. She was different. Practical. She winked with a vivid blue-lidded eye as she said, "Doncha worry, darling. No wedding day is perfect. Something will go wrong. It always does."

I almost leaned away, trying to escape this pronouncement, like Maleficent weaving a curse over the infant Sleeping Beauty.

Tina cleared her throat to cut her off, arms crossed. And Tina rarely got snippy with anyone.

The woman waved her kabuki brush. "Oh, it will be all right. It won't matter. Might be the chicken runs out. Or a groomsman loses his boutonniere. But the vows will happen. Happiness will win out, I promise." She dabbed my cheek.

I wondered what would go wrong today.

Eventually, I made it back to my bedroom and got helped into my dress by Tina. She went to fetch Vinnie and my father. We were going to do "first look" father and daughter photos.

I stood by the lace curtains in my bedroom window, the sun streaming over my veil, when the door opened.

Vinnie scooted in first, camera in hand. He'd worked for me for almost two years as an assistant shooter. "You look gorgeous, Mija."

He grinned at me from below a fat black mustache. His hair was glossy, plumped in front, and he wore a black jumpsuit with a big, pointed collar. He called himself Mexican Elvis and moonlighted as a lookalike in shows around town when we weren't shooting. Working weddings in this getup got him lots of Elvis gigs.

I didn't mind. I adored him. He'd been a good friend to Tucker and me since I'd left the big studio where I'd trained and struck out on my own. We'd met in photography class.

Vinnie had married his great love, Armando, last summer. I'd taken those photos.

He was the only person I trusted with my own big day. When I'd told him I was getting married, he had laughed. "Girl, if you could do the whole thing with selfies, you would."

He wasn't wrong. I did have a rather exacting look I wanted from my images.

Dad backed into the room to avoid seeing me too soon. "I might be too old to walk without looking." He held out his arms for balance, like a tall, gray-suited scarecrow.

"You're fine, Dad," I told him. "Just a few steps more."

"Circle around on three, Dad," Vinnie said. "One, two, *three.*"

Dad turned.

He sucked in a breath, his eyes misting over.

This made mine smart, too.

Dad held out his arms. "My beautiful daughter."

I walked into his embrace. Vinnie snapped the shots. I was careful not to smear the makeup artist's careful work on his shoulder.

"Got it," Vinnie said. "Gorgeous."

When I pulled away, I asked, "Can I see?" It was pointless, but I tried anyway.

Vinnie held the camera close to his chest. "No way, boss lady. This is my gig today."

"Okay, okay." I smoothed the lace across my bodice. It was already irritating my skin. Everything about the wedding was fancier than I liked, but Dad wanted to go all out. Ceremony on the green at the Barton Creek Country Club, a sit-down dinner after.

When he'd first laid out the plans, I'd balked. Was he trying to make up for the decade of my life he had missed?

Or that my mother wasn't allowed to attend?

Dad had insisted that no, this was what he'd always wanted for me, for all three of his girls.

It felt extravagant. Tucker and I lived simply. This dress alone cost the equivalent of two months' rent.

"You're calculating money in your head again," Dad said. "I can tell."

Guilty.

I couldn't help that I kept a running tally of expenses all the time. I'd been completely on my own when I turned eighteen, living in a women's shelter to escape my mother. It had been terrifying, not knowing the basics of normal life, like how to use a cell phone and being thrust into the world of rent, utility bills, and holding down a job.

The fear was imprinted on my soul and tattooed on my hip, the words angled so I could read them.

Mom is bad.

Vinnie slid closer, kneeling near my feet. I recognized

one of our signature shots, getting below the bouquet and showing the bride's face above her flowers.

My half sisters, Amanda and Jennifer, slipped into the room. They were my only bridesmaids and wore fitted dresses that floated to the floor in light pink chiffon. They had chosen them. I'd had no idea what to suggest.

Jennifer looked impish at eighteen, her pale hair a riot of perfectly spiraling curls. We'd celebrated her high school graduation a few weeks ago.

Amanda, home for the summer from Tulane, was tan and chic, with a smooth French twist.

Both of my sisters were so much more elegant than me. They took after their mother.

I prayed I never took after mine.

"Ava!" Jennifer cried. "You look so beautiful!"

Vinnie held up a hand. "Don't get in my frame."

"We won't!" Amanda backed away.

Tina stepped inside the room. "Can I come in?"

"Of course!" I called.

Vinnie sighed. "I suppose we have the shot."

I dropped the pose and wrapped an elbow around his neck. "It's fine. You're amazing." I tried to peek at the screen on the back of the camera, but he held it away.

"No cheating, Mija."

Busted.

"I need a photo with us all," I said. "Amanda, Jennifer, Dad, Tina. Come on!"

Vinnie waved us forward. "Yes, before everyone gets sweaty."

"It'll be fine," Tina assured us. "This June has been nice."

"It hit ninety today," Dad said.

"Oh, Dad, always complaining about Texas weather."

Jennifer pinched his arm in his light gray suit. "Don't say one bad thing about Ava's big day."

He cleared his throat. "I stand corrected. It's a gorgeous ninety degrees."

We smiled for Vinnie, who stood up on a chair to get a good angle.

He checked his watch as he jumped down. "It's time! Is the limo here?"

Jennifer ran to the window. "It's down there!"

I looked over her shoulder at the long white car on the street. I knew it was a staple for weddings, and truly, it was practical with six of us travelling at once.

But my mind still totaled the cost.

Two months of groceries.

Dad lifted my train and laid it over his arm as our group passed through my rented house. The rooms were clean and orderly even though they showed their age in the layers of paint and the scarred wood floor.

The entryway walls were covered with images. Me with Tucker, our heads close together, sun streaming through the leaves. Tucker working on the car, peering from under the open hood, a lopsided grin aimed at me.

Other pictures showed Tucker and Gram. Me with my father, my sisters. Roses. Oak trees. Squirrels from the yard. The Austin skyline.

My gaze slid along them. My life. I was taking the next step.

We walked out into the heat. The sidewalk was lined with dark pink vinca, the yellow daffodils long since faded from spring.

Vinnie hurried ahead to photograph us leaving the house, then ducked inside the limo to get shots of us entering.

Jennifer paused by the door, taking a selfie with her fingers in a peace sign.

"For my Insta," she said. "I didn't get a limo for prom." She shot Dad a look.

"I didn't get a limo for prom either," Dad said.

Jennifer sighed, turning her bouquet around in her hands. "That was the Stone Age."

He chuckled. "Right. The Stone Age of the eighties."

When the door closed and the driver strapped in, I let out a long sigh. Almost there.

The morning had started so early. The appointments. A light brunch with the women of the family, catered at my tiny table, the meal feeling too fancy for the warped cabinets and mismatched dishes.

My reconnection with my dad a few years ago had been good, but it was hard to keep my simple life separate from his opulent one. I'd lost so much, over and over again, that wealth felt like a burden. Something to slip through my fingers.

I wanted everything I cared about to fit in a bag. Every important moment to be documented in one easy-to-find place.

I fiddled with the bouquet. Marrying Tucker was the right thing. He'd always protected me, knowing from our first meeting that my mother was someone he would need to rescue me from. He'd nearly gone to jail for it.

And now we were here. Making it official.

I pressed my palm to the blooms, reveling in the cool, delicate petals. My fingers trembled.

Was I nervous? Of course not. Marrying Tucker was the best thing I could imagine.

But an alarm went off in my chest. Something was

wrong. I held up my hand. The tremor was growing, moving up to my wrist.

My arm dropped to the seat, no longer under my control.

Dad snapped to attention at the thud of my hand on the leather. "Ava?"

I realized with a jolt that I never took my seizure meds this morning. The most important part of my day. The most critical.

They were back in the cabinet over the boxes of leftover pastries from our decadent brunch.

I forgot about them. I was off schedule. Off routine.

I opened my mouth to tell my father, but it was too late. I couldn't speak.

"Ava?" Dad asked. "Are you okay?"

I wasn't.

A mechanical whine buzzed in my head. My vision grew dim in degrees, like someone was punching a button to turn the brightness down.

"That's a seizure," Dad said. "Damn it." He grasped my shoulders as I began to tilt.

I could still think, although everything moved in slow motion. Maybe it would be short. Maybe it wouldn't generalize to my whole body.

But as I listed sideways into my father's arms, I knew I would not get lucky here.

This one would be bad.

Something will go wrong. It always does. The makeup artist had predicted it.

But this time it wouldn't be okay.

My seizures differed from most. They caused complete amnesia. My entire memory got erased.

Tucker. My love. My rescuer.

My father, my sisters, Vinnie.

In a moment, I wouldn't remember who anyone was.

As the blackness took over, I tried to hold them in my mind.

Tucker. Father. Amanda. Jennifer.

I said their names over and over inside my head.

I couldn't forget them.

I couldn't start over.

Not today. Not on my wedding day.

Surely, I could hold on.

But then, it all winked out.

CHAPTER 3

Tucker

Something was wrong.

I waited in a small meeting room at the country club. It had a view of the green, where the wedding would be held.

The guests had assembled, sitting on white chairs beneath a large pavilion to protect them from the late afternoon sun.

Fans in each corner blew a fine mist over the rows.

"You seem nervous all of a sudden," Bill said, his hands clasped behind his back in a sharp black tux.

"Ava said she would text when they arrived, but it's ten minutes until we walk out, and she hasn't."

Bill moved closer, our ghosted reflections side by side. I barely recognized us, all spit-shined and formal. We hadn't looked like this since prom.

"Maybe she forgot. You know Vinnie is taking a million pictures. She probably doesn't have her phone with her. Wedding gowns don't exactly have pockets."

I was sure he was right, but at the same time, Ava knew how I worried. And a day like today was extra risky for her. For me, too, for that matter. Stress and seizures liked to walk the same path.

We'd had a good run since Ava's new med a few years ago. That was why she was willing to get married. She hadn't forgotten who I was in a long time, hadn't wanted me to move out, to avoid her having to live with a stranger.

Things were good.

I hoped they were still good.

She was never late. Never left me hanging about her whereabouts, her safety. Not in all the weddings she'd photographed or the times she went to Houston to see her father.

Fuentes entered the room, holding three beers. "Libations to get us through the ceremony. Bottoms up, pendejos."

Drinking was about the last thing I wanted to do right now, but I took one and pretended to take a swig to humor him.

Fuentes downed half of his in one go, nodding as he looked around the room. "This place is swank. It's an open bar, right? Damn, this is going to be a fun night."

Bill glanced my way, and I shrugged. Maybe Fuentes wasn't an ideal choice for a groomsman. I guess I could have gone with Big Harry. But Fuentes was the coworker who made Jiffy Lube bearable. He'd been around long enough to know what I'd gone through with Ava. Loving her even when she didn't know me.

I checked my phone for the hundredth time. "Should I text her?"

"Sure," Bill said. "But we're down to the wire."

We waited by the window. Jules, the wedding coordinator, headed toward the back door, treading carefully over the turf in her break-neck heels. Ava's dad had hired her to attend to all the details, not wanting Ava to feel any anxiety about the day.

"Go grab her and see if she's checked in with Ava," I told Bill. "She knows everything."

"I'll say," Fuentes said. "I didn't even have to tell her my shoe size. She already had it down. She's freaky as hell." He peered into his empty bottle. "Hot, though. I'd tap that."

Bill headed for the door right as my phone buzzed.

"Hold up," I said.

It was a message from Ava's dad.

Marcus: Seizure. Still down. In limo.

My stomach fell. I dropped onto a chair.

Me: How long?

It was a moment before another text came through, this time from his wife, Tina.

Tina: 3 minutes. It's bad. She's blue. We're headed to the hospital.

I set the beer bottle on the side table. Fuck. That was too long. She was going to lose her memory.

I wasn't worried about her dying. We'd been through this before. But the aftermath was a nightmare. Ava was a fighter at her core. She'd refuse help. Fake what she knew.

And she'd reject me. Three of the five times, she'd run from me. She trusted no one. No matter how I tried to convey my love for her, how I was safe, I never seemed to play it just right in those first hours after a seizure.

Jules entered the room. "It looks like the bride is delayed?"

I hadn't said anything to them yet. Bill watched me intently, probably sensing something had gone wrong.

Fuentes was taking in her short skirt.

There was no way to sugarcoat this. "Ava's on the way to the hospital."

Jules's face paled beneath her bright makeup. "Oh my God. Is she okay?"

I stood. I had to go. "She had a seizure in the limo. They're rerouting to the hospital to have her checked."

Jules pulled out her phone. "If she'll be here later, we can move up the cocktail hour, swap it for the wedding. The guests can have the dinner, and we could do the ceremony at the end."

I shook my head. "No, it's worse than that."

Jules looked up from her screen. "Oh, God. Will she be admitted? It's not…fatal, is it?"

Bill whirled on her. "It's not fatal. Jesus."

"She doesn't know." I walked toward the door, tapping out a response to Tina.

Me: I'll get Gram and head there. Which one?

Tina: Seton Central.

The usual. I shoved the phone into my pocket. "Jules, do what you want. Have the cocktails. The dinner. No sense wasting it. But there won't be a wedding today."

Jules straightened to full height, as if she were bracing herself. "I understand. I'll make the announcement. Will you come back?"

Would I? "I'm not sure. Just…just have a good time. I need to get Gram."

"I'll help out here," Bill said. "Keep me looped in."

I tugged on the door. "Thanks. I'll update you when I see her."

"Hey."

I stopped and turned to him.

Bill's face was grim. "You think she's lost it all?" He undoubtedly remembered the first time Ava lost her memory. She disappeared for months, and he'd found her first, working in a grocery store as if she'd never known any of us.

I frowned. "I don't know. But given that it's already been three minutes and they're headed to Seton, probably so."

His mouth drooped. "Sucks, man."

I nodded. "Yeah."

My footsteps in the rented shoes squeaked on the shiny floor as I headed toward the back exit to the green. I didn't want to say anything to anyone but Gram. Jules could handle it.

The crowd quieted as I walked over to where Gram sat in the front row with our close friends, Maya and Big Harry.

"You were supposed to come from the side," Gram said. "Change of plans?" Then she took in my face. "Oh, no. It happened?" She knew my fear. Worry about Ava had been a constant for us since the beginning.

I nodded. "They took her to Seton. We need to go."

Maya leaned forward, concern etched into the wrinkles of her smooth, brown face. "What can we do?"

"I guess let everyone know. Have dinner, maybe?"

She patted my hand. "Don't worry about us. Harry and I have got this."

I helped Gram get to her feet. I wanted to hurry, to rush to Ava, but there would be no point.

By the time we got to the hospital, the seizure would be over. Ava would be sitting in a room with her father and stepmother and sisters. She'd be lost, possibly defensive, probably trying to hide her confusion.

And all of us would have become total strangers.

CHAPTER 4

Ava

Everything itched.

Opening my eyes to see what was scratching my neck and arms was too painful. The light blinded me instantly, so I squeezed them shut again.

My fingers closed over the rough fabric at my collarbone and tore it away.

That was better.

A voice cried, "Ava! Your dress!"

I didn't know who it was or who they were talking to or why they were so upset, so I ignored it. I needed to work on whatever was irritating my upper arms.

I worked the fabric between my thumb and first finger, and the word for it arrived.

Lace.

Right. Lace itched.

Another voice said, "She's ruining her gown."

They were talking about me. The tone made my stomach quiver. I pressed my hand there, willing it to stop. It was uncomfortable and made me feel jittery.

But my body wasn't still. I was lying down on something, but the something was *moving*. It bounced, and my head lifted, then slammed onto the floor.

"Owwwwww."

"Marcus, cushion her head." The first voice.

I bloomed with pain. I squinted as hard as I could and peeked at my surroundings.

Five faces peered down at me. All their expressions made the jittery feeling get worse, so I closed my eyes again.

"Go away," I said, covering my eyes with one hand and holding out the other.

Another voice, deeper than the others. "Ava, I'm your father. Do you know what a father is?"

I did. Somehow. I sensed connection. Mother and father and children. Who was *my* father?

I had no idea, and this made the panic increase. I should know my father. Why didn't I know? My heart thudded hard in my chest, increasing the pressure in my head with each *thump, thump, thump.*

Something squeezed my shoulder, startling me. I scooted backward, trying to use my feet to move.

But there was something on my feet—shoes, I guessed, strange and spiky and hard to move in.

"Ava," the first voice said. "We're almost at the hospital."

Hospital. That was for sick people.

Yes, that would be good. I was clearly sick. Nothing felt right, a hundred alarms sounding all over my body.

The itching was the least of my problems. My head hurt so badly that my stomach was revolting. I didn't know what would come after this heaving, but it had to be bad.

I managed to roll over and get to my knees. I was

trapped in layers of fabric. With my head facing down, I could open my eyes more easily. The floor was dark, with no light shining directly at me, no faces that made my stomach react.

But I couldn't control my breath. The air rattled in my throat.

"Breathe, Ava," the voice of the person claiming to be my father was gentler now. "You're hyperventilating. You're okay. We're here. We will help you."

These words soothed me, making my belly stop its lurching. I sucked in a long gulp of air.

I couldn't talk. I had nothing to say. I didn't know the questions to ask. I stayed on my hands and knees, shifting from right to left to adjust to the movements of the floor.

I lifted my head. We were inside a car, a big car. The seats ran along both sides, facing each other. A driver sat in the front, the window between his part of the car and ours rolled halfway down.

"She okay?" the man called.

"We're stable," the father person said. "Just pull into emergency."

We drove past row after row of cars in every color. A brown building appeared with a huge red cross over the door.

The father kneeled in front of me. "Your name is Ava. You're my daughter. You had a seizure. You probably feel very confused. We're here to help."

I stared at his face. He had brown hair mixed with gray and a thick mustache trimmed in a neat, even line.

My throat hurt, but I said, "My head."

He nodded. "We'll get you something for the pain. Can you sit on the seat?" He reached for my arm.

"I think so."

He lifted me until I was upright and on the cushion. I realized I was in a long, heavy white dress. Three women were also in long dresses, all pink.

Another man with a mustache touched his forehead, chest, and shoulders. "Dios mío, I thought we'd lost you, Mija."

I got lost?

The car stopped in front of a long wall of glass. "I'll go ahead and tell them the situation," the father said. "Tina, you and the girls wait here with Ava."

I clasped my hands in my lap, realizing that if I squeezed tightly, it helped the pain in my head.

The four faces watched me intently. Even the driver was turned around, like I was something strange and foreign to be examined.

My head felt empty, the sights and sounds and words since I woke on the floor rattling around. I focused on each moment. The car. The light. The pain. The lace. The big, heavy dress. I didn't know what any of it meant.

The father returned with two other men. "We're going to get you out, Ava." He ducked inside and took my hands to help me across the car to the door.

The world was so bright I had to close my eyes again. I allowed the men to seat me in a wheelchair.

"Don't let her dress get caught," one of them said.

The chair moved.

I scrunched my eyes to see us rolling toward the sliding door.

We bumped up a short ramp with ridges that made my head ache. Suddenly, my feet felt different. One was not like the other.

I looked down but couldn't see anything under all the dress.

I pulled and pulled on the skirt to find my feet. Had one of them been injured?

When I revealed them, one was bare, and the other was encased in a white shoe.

I glanced behind me.

The other shoe sat on the ramp, fallen on its side, sharp and bright against the brown sidewalk.

It was as alone and lost as I was.

CHAPTER 5

Tucker

Gram clasped her hand over mine in the center console as I drove her old Buick to the hospital. It was well out of the way of the route between our house and the country club, but Marcus would have wanted to go there to access Ava's records.

We hadn't been in this awful position for years. Not since we'd struggled to find a new med for her after the one that was preventing her seizures ended up causing liver damage.

Three memory resets in a row were impossibly hard. Each time it happened, I had to win her over all over again. She always wanted me to move out and give her space.

Gram knew the direction of my thoughts. "You've done it before. You can do it again."

I realized I didn't have the laptop with the videos we'd prepared back when we were going through this before. Even so, they weren't up to date. Nothing in there explained we lived together and were getting married.

We'd been complacent, lulled into how easy life had been the last few years.

Still, it was something. In the sequence, Ava explains to herself who she is, who I am, her father, Gram, Maya, Big Harry. All the important players. She also warns herself about her mother.

Shortly after the last reset three years ago, we went to all the places that jogged sensory memories, the parts of her brain that could connect feelings to location, which she insisted helped her reorient herself. The children's hospital, Big Harry's Diner, Maya's flower-covered front porch.

Visiting them in person was best because a creaky door or the smell of fried food or the roughness of the terrain were the best ways to help her brain find safety in the terrifying nothingness she described as having her memories erased. But that took convincing her to go.

Not always easy when survival Ava arrived.

"I should go get the sequence videos," I told Gram. "Without them, there's no telling what direction she might go."

"But we're almost to the hospital," she said. "Let's see how she is and go from there."

She was right. Besides, almost half an hour had passed. The version of Ava that was going to present itself would already be established.

She'd never woken up with her father, not since she was a little girl. Normally, I was there.

Maybe that would make the difference.

Maybe I was the problem.

We pulled up to the emergency room doors. "I'll drop you off and catch up after I've parked," I told Gram.

"Are you sure?"

"Yes. Text me if you find them."

She opened her door. "I will."

Something glinted on the curb. I almost ignored it, but it's familiarity caught my eye.

I leaned over the console as Gram stood up. "Is that Ava's shoe?"

She bent down to pick it up. "I think it is." She passed it to me.

I held the shiny white heel. It wasn't midnight, and I wasn't exactly a prince, but I'd take any symbol I could get.

Even though the Ava I loved would be physically fine, sitting on an exam table in the ER, nothing about her would be the same.

She might be hostile. Or terrified. Or frantic. We'd seen all those versions of her after she'd emerged from a seizure of this magnitude.

Gram closed the door, and I pulled forward to enter the parking garage.

The doctors would never listen to me, at least not until we got in touch with her usual neurologist. Memory loss like Ava's was extremely rare, although losing a half-hour before a seizure was typical. It used to happen to me.

But in the ER, they always dismissed our concerns and left us to deal with it on our own. This time, though, we had the father factor.

I might be a minor character in the new world of Ava. And technically, I still wasn't her husband.

The Buick barely fit between a pillar and an SUV, but I squeezed through the door and made a dead run for the stairs with the shoe in my hand.

I wasn't clear why people stopped to stare as I passed, other than my speed, until I caught sight of myself in the glass panes leading to emergency.

Full tux. Boutonniere. A fancy shoe. They'd think we were doing a Cinderella-inspired flash mob or a viral video prank.

I spotted Gram at the desk, flanked by Ava's sisters Jennifer and Amanda, plus Vinnie, Ava's photography assistant. They all looked terribly out of place in their fancy clothes. The other patients in the chairs watched with interest. A few not-so-covertly filmed them with their phones.

"Only two people can go back," Amanda said. "Mom is going to come out so you can go."

The secure doors whooshed open to the right of the desk, and Tina emerged, looking poised as always. I wasn't sure anything rattled her. "She's awake. Go straight back and find the section on the left. She's behind the third curtain."

"How is she?" Gram asked.

Tina's lips pressed into a glossy rose-colored line. "Curled up in a ball. Won't talk."

Terrified Ava. I wasn't sure whether this version would be easier or harder than before.

"Thanks," I told Tina. "I'll report back."

"Tucker," Vinnie said. "Hold up."

I paused and turned to him. He looked grim in his shiny black pantsuit. He passed me the fancy camera.

"I don't know how to use it," I told him. And why would I want to take pictures?

He turned it aside and showed me a play button. "She had me hold on to a recording on a memory card she made in case something happened while we were together. It's been in my camera case ever since." He pressed play.

I watched the screen. Ava sat on a chair in the spare

bedroom, which she used as her office, dressed like she always was in jeans and a T-shirt. This one read, "I'm about to snap."

She gave a little wave. "Hey, Ava, I'm you. If you're not sure, look at this tattoo." She held up her arm, showing off the words inked there. "Go ahead, find it."

Vinnie pressed stop. "Hopefully, it will help."

I held the camera against my chest. "Thanks."

A nurse came out of the secure doors, so I hurried through while they were open. Time to find out what I was dealing with.

The curtain to the third sectioned room was closed, so I paused to listen for a second in case it was the wrong one.

Then I heard Marcus. "Ava, this is a photograph of you as a young girl."

He still carried her kindergarten picture. I wasn't surprised because him having it when Ava had met with him after a decade apart was what had turned the tide of their estrangement.

There was no way to knock, so I cleared my throat and said, "It's Tucker."

The curtain moved aside. Marcus held it back to let me in.

Ava sat at the far end of a hospital bed, her knees drawn up to her chin. The white fabric of her dress spilled to the edges of the mattress, piling up inside the plastic rails.

I knew not to approach too quickly or to touch her. I stopped at the end of the bed. "Hello, Ava. I'm Tucker."

She peered at me with wide, frightened eyes. Her hair had been swept into an intricate updo, fixed with rhinestone combs. It was now only half up, the rest flowing over her shoulders.

Ava never wore makeup, so this flawless version of her with creamy skin and lined eyes and long lashes took some getting used to. She was heartbreakingly beautiful and so scared.

"Does anything hurt?" I asked her.

"They gave her some ibuprofen for her head," Marcus said.

I spotted her other shoe on the floor and set the matching one beside it. "I found this outside," I said.

"I wondered where it went," Marcus said.

I knew better than to do too much talking without involving Ava. It irritated her whether or not she'd had a seizure.

Her gaze moved to the camera in my hands. She tilted her head with curiosity.

For a split second, I almost wanted her mother before shunting that thought away. From Ava's notes and talking to Maya, who had lived next door to Ava and her mother for years, sometimes Ava's memory loss was so complete she could no longer read or write.

I had never seen that level of disability, and I didn't know the signs.

I cleared my throat. "This camera has a video on it that you recorded so you could talk to yourself when you were scared."

Her eyes lifted to watch my face.

I made sure to give her a kind, easy expression. "Would you like me to press play so you can listen?"

She looked back at the camera, which I took to mean she was interested.

I set the camera on the end of the bed and pressed the play button Vinnie had shown me.

Thankfully, the video started over.

"Hey, Ava, I'm you. If you're not sure, look at this tattoo. Go ahead, find it."

Ava's gaze immediately moved to her arms. Her wedding gown was short-sleeved, so it was easy to spot the tattoo.

"Can you read it?" the recording asked.

This was good. Ava had already predicted what her future self would need.

Ava nodded at the recording as if her former self were there.

"Say it out loud," the recording said.

"Trust only this handwriting," Ava said from the bed. "Find the book. Remember your life."

I released some of the tension I was holding in my chest. She could understand. She could read. She could talk.

The recording went on. "Ava, if you can't read it, you need big help. Look at the faces of the people around you and trust yourself to know who is there to help you and who isn't. Always trust this feeling. It will steer you right."

Ava glanced at us briefly, then returned to watching the video.

"If you could read it, let's move on. You should have gotten this recording from Vinnie. He has black hair, and he's kind of short. He is a good one. See, here he is."

Vinnie's voice says, "Hola, Mija."

Uh, oh. We broke protocol on this.

Ava's eyes flew to me. "You're not Vinnie," she said. Then to her father. "You're not Vinnie."

"Look at us, Ava," I said quickly. "You told yourself to trust your feelings."

She crawled to the top of the bed again, this time snatching up the camera. "Where is Vinnie?"

"I'll send him in," Marcus said and exited the curtain.

"Look at me," I said to Ava. "I love you."

She curled her arm around the camera, which was still talking. "Go away. I want Vinnie."

I heard my name on the recording, but Ava wasn't listening.

"Hey, you talked about me. Listen." I moved forward to see if I could figure out how to rewind that part, but Ava recoiled.

"You scare me," she said. Her eyes flitted to the tattoo. "Where is my book?"

"I can get it for you. It's at our house."

She turned on the bed to face the back curtain, curling over the camera. Her dark hair streamed down her back, falling from the sparkly combs. The recording continued. "Vinnie and I work together with this very camera. You take photographs. Vinnie helps."

"You help," Ava repeated. She stayed hunched over the screen, ignoring me. The two of them in the video talked about photography and kidded each other, establishing their friendship.

So, that's how this one would go. Vinnie would be the star of this version of Ava.

I had my work cut out for me.

CHAPTER 6

Ava

The screen in front of me talked, and I was on it! When it ended, I wanted to hear it again, but the other person was still behind me. He'd said his name, but I couldn't remember what it was.

I pushed on different parts of the camera, but I couldn't figure out which one made the screen work.

"Do you need some help?" he asked, but I ignored him.

He was bigger than me, and so was the other man who said he was my father. I didn't know either of them. They could be lying.

The only thing I knew was that Vinnie was good. And that I should trust only the handwriting on my arm. I needed the book to remember my life.

"Ava! My girl! How are you?"

I turned around. This was the voice from my video.

The man was dressed all in shiny black, but his face and hair were the same as the recording.

"Vinnie?"

"Yes, Mija, yes." He approached the side of the bed. "Why is my Ava facing the wall? Come here." He helped me turn around. "You always told me you might forget me, and here, I thought I was unforgettable."

"What's happening, Vinnie?"

"Did you watch the whole video?"

I shook my head, glancing over at the other man. "I tried." I held the camera tightly against my chest. I wanted to wear something else. Everything about this dress itched. I yanked the lace across my neck again.

Vinnie noticed. "Girl, today is your wedding day. You're marrying that one." He pointed at the other man. "Everybody you know is sitting at the club waiting for you. Poor Mija."

The word Mija settled into my bones. It was more familiar than anything else anyone had said.

"Am I Mija?" I asked.

He smiled. "You are to me. Did you understand that? Mi palabra favorita?"

"Si," I said. "Mija. Not Ava."

Vinnie glanced at the other man, the one I was supposed to marry today. "You are Mija to me. But your name is Ava." He seemed less happy now, a frown making a line form between his eyebrows. "What do you remember?"

I wasn't sure how to answer that. I knew the word remember. And I knew what he meant. But I couldn't find a way to answer the question. It was like I was trying to move a part of my body that wouldn't work.

"Do you remember meeting me before today?" Vinnie asked.

"No," I said, squeezing my eyes shut to focus on the images there. "I can see the limo. The itchy dress." I tugged on it again. "The man who said he is my father." I glanced at the other man. "This one."

"Tucker," that man said. "I'm Tucker."

"Hold on," Vinnie said. "I have pictures from earlier today. Let me switch out the cards." He took the camera from me and opened a little compartment. A small black rectangle popped out.

He reached for the strap across his chest. He removed another rectangle from inside it and pushed it into the camera.

This was all so fascinating. "Can I do that?" I asked.

Vinnie hesitated, as if I had said something wrong. But then he said, "Sure." He pointed to the tiniest button. "Push that."

I pushed it, and the rectangle popped out. "I did it!" I felt like laughing. Then I pressed the rectangle back in. "What is that?"

Vinnie glanced over at Tucker, his frown back. "It's the memory card. You don't know what it is?"

"I've never seen one before. How does it help your memory?" I could use that, whatever it is.

Vinnie's eyes looked into mine, and suddenly, I felt much less happy than I did when I pushed out the rectangle. I sat back, moving away from him.

Tucker leaned forward against the foot of the bed. "Hey. It's okay. Vinnie has never seen you lose your memory. He's adjusting."

I looked at Tucker. He also seemed upset. He had the same crease between his eyebrows.

I pushed the camera away and scooted to the top of the bed, drawing up my knees. Nothing was working. My stomach felt hot and sick.

"Where is my book?" I asked them. "I need my book to remember my life."

Vinnie looked to Tucker, his frown deeper. My belly quaked. They were unhappy. What would they do?

Tucker spoke up. "Ava, we have the book at home. I am happy to show it to you. And we have lots more videos for you to watch. They will help you feel better. Do you want to feel better?"

I did. But Ava on the screen told me to trust my feelings, and my feelings were scared again. I covered my eyes. It was too much. Too many voices. Too much information. I needed quiet. And calm.

Vinnie took a step back from the bed. "Should we get the doctor?"

"It's a Saturday," Tucker said. "We won't get the one who understands her condition. As soon as they see she's not in any danger, they will discharge us."

Vinnie let out a long, slow breath. That had to be bad. It didn't sound normal.

I moved my hands to my ears and shut my eyes. I didn't want to hear anything else or see anything more. I wanted quiet. Blackness. That peace I'd felt before the bright light in the car, then people, the rolling chair.

I wanted out of this itchy dress.

I wanted…something. I didn't know exactly what else. But not this. Not this. Not this.

Tears leaked out of my eyes. My nose started tingling. I bent over, my head in my lap, but the dress had sparkly parts that cut into my skin.

That was enough. I tore at the skirt, the sleeves. I wanted it off.

"We'd better find her something else to wear," Vinnie said.

"Ava, let me help," Tucker said. He approached the

side of the bed and touched my back, but I twisted, elbows out, to keep him away.

"Go get her dad," Tucker said. "He will talk to the nurses. Maybe we will need a sedative. It's never been this bad."

I didn't like them talking about me this way, so I kept jerking side to side, elbows flying. Tucker's hands were on my back, doing something.

I let out a low, angry roar at him, but then my back felt better.

I dropped my elbows. The dress was falling away, coming off at the front.

"Just one more button," Tucker said.

Then it was free. I pulled it forward, off me.

Relief flooded my body. I pressed my hands to my neck. The terrible itch was gone.

"Here," Tucker said. "Let me cover you."

I looked down. I wasn't wearing anything under the dress.

Tucker took off his jacket and wrapped it around me. It was rough, but so much softer than the dress. I held it tightly.

The father person returned with a woman in blue clothes. She came to my side. "Ava, are you feeling agitated?"

"It was the dress," Tucker said. "I think she'll be better with it off."

"I'll go find her something to wear," Dad said. "Surely, there's a shop close by."

"You can get sweats in the gift shop. Longhorn stuff, Texas stuff, you know." The woman tapped on a big screen in her hand. "I'll see if we can get the doctor in here."

The father person left, then the nurse.

Tucker stood by the bed. "You want me to help you get the dress the rest of the way off? There's a paper sheet to cover yourself until your dad finds some pants."

"Yes."

He helped me off the bed, and the dress fell to the ground. I wore white panties.

But more words caught my eye.

On one of my hips was the name Ava Roberts and numbers. 7-7-00.

I rubbed at them. They were like my arm —a tattoo.

Tucker looked up from where he was unfolding a big blue paper sheet. "That's your name and birthday. You wanted to be able to remember it."

"Oh."

Then I spotted the other side. "Mom is bad." My head buzzed, and a ringing filled my ears. I covered them, but the noise was inside. "Tucker?"

He moved close and wrapped his arms around me. "We got you away from your mom. You're safe. We've got you."

For a moment, his arms felt right, like I belonged there. Then he let go and wrapped the blue sheet around my waist, tucking it in so it would stay.

"Vinnie said there is a wedding?" I managed to say. "You and me? Married?"

"We were supposed to," he said. "I understand you don't know me anymore. I've been through this before."

"With me?"

This smile matched his face. "Yes, only with you." He pulled a screen of his own from his pocket. As he tapped on it, something connected about the device. It was a phone.

He clicked on one of several colorful squares. "This is our house."

I peered at it. A blue building sat on a green lawn with yellow flowers leading up to the door.

"Right now, there are pink flowers instead." He tapped the row of blooms.

"Did I plant them?"

"You did. You love tending flowers. And photographing them."

This was interesting. I searched my thoughts for feelings about flowers but couldn't find any. "Can I see other photos?"

"Of course." He flipped through one after another. A street. Two kids walking a dog. A bunch of skies in different colors. Then, a woman.

"Is that me?" I took the phone.

"Yes. A couple of weeks ago."

"Does your picture talk?"

He touched the screen, and it went away, replaced by lots of little squares. "Not that one. But this one does."

The picture moved like the one in the camera. It was me in front of the blue house. I was holding a long green wire. A hose. A water hose. Water sprayed out of the end. "I'm going to get you, Tucker!" I said.

Water hit the screen, making me lean away. But of course, it couldn't get to me. It was only a video.

Tucker's voice said, "Not the phone!" There was a blur of sky, and then the video ended.

The colors and sounds made me smile. I touched my lips. Was that the instinct I talked about? "I live with you?"

Tucker nodded. "We live in the blue house together." He frowned. "I don't know if you were off schedule or if you forgot to take your pills, or maybe the excitement of the day got to you, but your seizure meds failed today."

His face became so sad that I could feel it changing my own feelings. "I don't think I can get married today."

"I know."

The curtains parted, and a new man in a white coat entered. "The bride and groom! I hear you got too excited today." He stepped too close, too fast, and I scooted to the far end of the bed.

He came around the side. "Don't be shy. I need to look at your pupils."

I couldn't remember *pupils*.

He leaned forward, and I leaned away.

"Look into the light."

It was bright, and pain pierced my head. I closed my eyes tightly.

"Is this typical behavior for her?" he asked. "Is she cognitively impaired?"

I didn't know what any of that meant.

Tucker said, "Her seizures hit the hippocampus. She's lost her procedural memory. She'll be pretty afraid. You're scaring her."

"Fascinating. You seem to know your stuff."

"Of course I do. I'm her husband. Or would have been."

I sensed the doctor leaning away and cautiously opened one eye. He had stepped back.

"I see she's a patient of Dr. Simmons. I assume you want me to refer her to his care? It sounds like a complex case."

"That's fine. We may need a med adjustment since she's had a breakthrough, but he will handle that."

"Good. I'll get the checkout papers initiated." He

clapped Tucker on the back. "Tough day for it." Then, he was gone.

I held the jacket together tightly. "Can I go to the blue house now? I want the book."

"Soon," Tucker said. "Your dad will get you some new clothes to put on, and we will sign some papers. Then, we'll get you home."

"And get the book?"

"Yes, we'll get the book." His eyes turned to my arm, where the tattoo was. I was glad the jacket covered it. It felt like a secret between the Ava on the video and me. Even if Tucker was nice enough, I didn't want him to see the handwriting that I had to trust.

I needed a break from the rush of noise and pain and sick feelings.

I wanted to get to that blue house with its flowers and its water hose. I needed the book. That was the only thing I knew to hope for in the little time I'd had so far.

CHAPTER 7

Tucker

When Ava was discharged, we led her out to the waiting room.

She wrapped her arms around her belly in the Longhorn sweats her father had brought. She didn't let anyone help her change.

She was barefoot, and I carried her wedding gown and shoes.

The family stood from their row of chairs when we passed through the sliding doors.

Marcus explained the situation. "Ava would like to go to her house. Tucker is going to orient her. I'll go with them. We can take Gram's car."

"What should we do?" Tina asked.

Jennifer and Amanda were hugging each other, distress on their faces. Vinnie stood near the back, not catching anyone's eye.

I got it. This was a lot. They'd seen too much, and it was hard to wrap your head around the idea that someone you knew so well and loved so hard didn't want to be near you.

"We could use some family at the country club to explain things," Marcus said. "Gram, are you up for that?"

"Of course," Gram said.

"How can we go without Ava?" Amanda cried. "What do we do without her?" Tears rolled down her face.

Ava turned away. I had to get her out of here. It was too much emotion. Ava hated that in the early days after a memory loss.

"We'll figure it out," Marcus said. "This is what we have to deal with. Tina, take them in the limo with Gram. Vinnie, is your car at Ava's?"

"Yeah, but I can go to the country club and get a ride back to my car. I should take a few pictures, you know, to document the day."

He wouldn't meet my gaze. I hoped Ava wasn't too hung up on him being her only friend. He clearly needed a minute to process all this.

She didn't seem to be. She had her back turned to all of us.

Gram drew me in for a hug, curving over the bulk of the wedding dress. "Hang in there, love. I'll update you from the club. Let me know if you need Maya or Harry."

"I will." I almost wished I could keep her with us. I needed an ally. But there was a lot to handle at the wedding site. Over an hour had passed. Heck, maybe everyone had left.

But there were people to pay, gratuities to hand out. Soon, a small band would arrive to play the song for our first dance.

I glanced at Ava. We had practiced that song a time or two, not that we were doing anything fancy.

Now, we wouldn't get to dance.

I fought against the tide of despair that threatened to drag me under. I couldn't afford it. Not now.

We filed out. At first, Ava didn't move, but Marcus touched her shoulder. "Let's get you where you want to go."

That got her. She followed us.

"I'll get the car. She doesn't have shoes." I didn't want to leave her, not even for a minute, but she couldn't walk through the parking garage with bare feet.

I hurried up the stairs, the miles of fabric slipping in my arms. I tossed the gown and shoes in the back seat before pulling off my tux jacket. It was hot and stiff. I didn't want these clothes anymore, either. I yanked the tie loose and piled it with everything else in the back.

When I sat behind the wheel, I intended to start the car and hurry to the entrance.

But emotion crashed over me in a wave of nausea. I'd lost her again. And this time, we lived together. Our paths were intertwined. I didn't have the luxury of waiting her out, approaching her slowly.

It had to go better this time. It had to.

I swiped at my eyes. No crying, Tucker. Not one minute.

For a terrifying moment, my own head sizzled. Shit. No. Not happening.

I didn't have the magnet on me that activated the VNS device implanted in my chest. But every sixty seconds, it would do its thing without it.

My hands gripped the steering wheel as I breathed slowly and evenly, willing myself calm. I counted to sixty once, then again.

I couldn't feel the gentle pulse of electricity that was generated by the device in my chest and went up a wire that wrapped around my vagus nerve in my neck. But it happened, nonetheless. This zap prevented a seizure from getting anywhere. Meds hadn't worked for me, but this device had given me my life back.

When I felt reasonably sure I was fine, I started the engine. Sweat poured from my hair and down my neck before trickling over my forehead from the stuffy interior. I should have cranked the AC first thing.

I tried to breathe evenly as I drove to the exit. I had to be chill for Ava. No emotions. Nothing for her to interpret negatively.

I had forgotten that leaving required a payment. I reached behind me for the jacket and dug for my wallet. By the time I got around to the exit, Ava was pacing back and forth in small, angry steps.

Marcus opened the passenger door. "Front or back?" he asked her.

She assessed the seats. "Back."

He opened the rear door and pushed the dress to one side.

Ava slid onto the seat, immediately pulling her knees to her chest.

Marcus closed the door and sat next to me. "Everything all right?"

"Yeah," I said, aiming a stream of cooled air to the back of the car.

I glanced at Ava in the rearview mirror from time to time as I drove us home. She stared out the window, sometimes sitting up to peer at something more intently.

I had no idea what it was like for her at these times, waking up in a foreign place, surrounded by strangers. She had no memories to comfort her, no experiences to guide her to what was safe or dangerous.

The doctors had explained over the years how hard this was on her system. To have a full vocabulary, to understand speech and language, but not to know what things truly meant. You could say, "Let's go to the park," and maybe she could conceptualize that you were suggesting going to a place, but she couldn't picture swings or grass. She had no idea what to expect when she got there.

Her singular focus at the moment was the book, thanks to the tattoo she got when she was eighteen. This worried me. In the string of resets she'd had after being forced to change meds a few years ago, we'd tried to refine the book.

The first one she'd assembled when she was eighteen was too frightening, full of warnings about her mother, men in general, and to trust no one. She'd prepared it after living at a women's shelter.

The next one had mainly photos to avoid the scary parts, but at her next reset, she hadn't had the patience to stare at the images and figure out who people were.

We determined that she needed something to grab her attention like her tattoo did, and we created a mixed scrap-book of warnings about her mother, plus images from her current life to prove to her who her allies were.

Except it wasn't current. We hadn't updated it in years.

Maybe she would watch the videos this time since she'd already seen one. They helped the most if we could get her to sit down with them. Ava always listened to herself intently once she realized who was talking to her.

Marcus turned to me. "We're almost there. Do you have a plan?"

I knew what he meant. "We'll try videos."

"I can hear you," Ava said. "I want the book."

We both frowned. Ava was smart. She wanted the handwriting that her tattoo talked about.

My phone buzzed. When we got to a light, I pulled it out.

It was Marcus.

Marcus: Did you fix that scrapbook? She ran from us over it before. We almost lost her.

He's right.

I glanced over at him. "It needs updating," I said.

He typed rapidly.

Marcus: Maybe I can distract her while you go through the book and fix it.

I nod. "Okay."

He could make her some food. I would say I'm going to go fetch it. And I'd make sure the book was in good shape before I gave it to her.

"I'll get the book," I told Marcus. "I'll bring it to the kitchen. Maybe you can get her something to eat."

The light turned green, so I set the phone down and focused on getting us home.

This had to work.

I needed this time to be easier.

CHAPTER 8

Ava

I took my time leaving the car and walking up the sidewalk to the blue house.

Pink flowers lined the path, just like Tucker had said.

Tucker ran ahead to unlock the yellow door. My father waited behind me, holding the itchy dress and painful shoes.

I didn't like being between them, and something urged me to escape, but I had nowhere to go. I was at their mercy.

The flowers were tall bursts of green topped with tiny blooms. I ran my hand along their petals, which tickled my palms. The sidewalk was warm beneath my feet. I inhaled slowly and carefully, then let the air go. It helped. I wondered how my body knew to do that.

Up ahead, Tucker opened the door and waited.

I wasn't ready to be trapped again, like I had been on the bed in the curtained room. I paused to look at a rock that was different from the other gray ones. It was bright blue. Then another, yellow.

The colored ones had numbers on top. 2018. 2019. 2021.

The last one was white and black. 2025. Something about this one drew me to it. I picked it up.

Now that I was looking more closely, I could see the white part had a pattern like my dress, and the black had a V of white in the middle like Tucker's suit.

"Each rock has a date for a significant part of our lives together," Tucker called out from his position near the door. "That one we put out yesterday for our wedding day." His mouth was grim, the corners turned down.

I glanced over the other rocks again. I wondered what was significant about the other dates. Maybe the book would tell me.

I couldn't see my tattoo because of the long sleeve of my sweatshirt. It was hot out, though, and the longer I stood in one place, the warmer I got.

I moved to the shade of the front door, although I stepped aside to avoid being too close to Tucker.

My father followed. "Are we ready to go in?"

Tucker looked at me.

"Okay," I said.

Tucker led the way. I followed him into a narrow space lined with photos. To the left was a bright white room with a blue sofa and a television.

I turned to the images. I spotted myself, although my hair in these pictures was longer than it was in the video I'd made with Vinnie. Vinnie was not in any of these photos, but many of them had Tucker. I also saw my father and the woman who'd been with him. Plus, the two other girls from the limo.

There was one with the tiny gray-haired woman from the waiting room.

I stared at all of them, trying to find meaning in any of the faces or scenes. Looking at them made me feel better than I had since waking up in the limo, though, so I kept doing it.

"You're a photographer," Tucker said. "Oh, right. Vinnie said that in the video. But you're really good. You took all of these, even the ones you're in."

I nodded. Maybe that was why they were so pleasing. They looked exactly the way I would have wanted them to.

Tucker took a step toward another room at the back, and the floor creaked. I startled at the sound and then laughed. "You should fix that!" I said in a voice I scarcely recognized, bright and happy.

I clapped my hand over my mouth. It had popped out without my thinking.

For a moment, Tucker smiled in a way that made his entire face beautiful. My stomach flipped. I smiled back, touching my cheeks. So many things were happening here that I didn't quite control.

"You always say that," he said. "I'll get to it, I promise."

"Is that typical?" my father asked. "For her to just say things she used to say?"

"Yeah," Tucker said, then turned to me. "If you're distracted or startled, there are things you do and say that are the same across all the memory losses."

That was interesting. So, something inside me was still me.

He kept walking toward the bright room. It was a kitchen lined with cabinets. A small table with metal legs and a white cloth on top sat in the middle. It was piled with boxes and flowers and small bags.

More boxes were piled on one cabinet.

"It's messy due to all the activity," Tucker said. "You

had your hair and makeup done in here, plus a brunch with Tina and your sisters. Normally, you like things very neat and orderly."

"We should check her meds," my father said. He folded the wedding dress over a chair and sat the shoes on the floor.

Tucker opened a cabinet and pulled down a purple plastic case. "We keep them organized by day so she never misses." He angled it toward us. "Saturday is in here. I guess in all the craziness, she forgot to take them."

My belly quivered. So, this was my fault? The way I was feeling, the missed wedding, the fear? Because I didn't take a pill?

I stumbled backward, running into the stove. When I pulled away, my sweatshirt caught on one of the knobs, making it turn. A *click-click* sound startled me, followed by a whiff of a new, sharp smell.

"That's the gas!" My father lunged at me.

I let out a shriek and dodged to the side, but he was aiming for the knob. He flipped it off and picked up a towel, flapping it in the air.

I was trapped by my father near the door to the hall where we'd come and Tucker on the other side. I could escape only if I ducked under the table.

That sounded good. I dove beneath it, pushing aside a chair to give me room. I pulled my knees up, pressing my face between them. Rocking back and forth was soothing, so I did it fiercely, trying to tune out anything happening in the room.

"Ava, I'm sorry. I had to turn off the gas on the stove." My father's voice was close, so he must have kneeled down.

"Let her have a moment," Tucker said. "This is over-whelming."

The room fell quiet. I breathed into my knees, my back already hurting from my cramped position. But I kept rocking.

"Ava, I'm going to get your book," Tucker said. "You can look at it down here."

I turned my head and opened my eyes. His shiny black shoes left the room. My father's were still here.

He pulled out a chair, and I almost bolted, but he sat down on it, a few feet from me. I watched his shoes and legs. One of his hands rested on a thigh, his thumb tapping rapidly.

Did that help? I tried it, resting my hand on my leg and thumping it with my thumb.

It didn't. I gave up and rocked some more until my butt started hurting, too.

Footsteps returned. Tucker's shiny shoes appeared. "Ava, I'm going to give you two things. One is the book so you can check the handwriting and remember your life. The other is your laptop computer, which is open to the video you made for yourself a few years ago the last time this happened. It's a better one than the one with Vinnie. It tells you more."

He sat down on the floor in front of me, but well away. He showed me a large book with a black-and-white cover. On the cover were the words:

Trust only this handwriting.
    This is the book.
    Remember your life.

• • •

My stomach quivered as he pushed it toward me. This was it. I shoved my sleeve up to my elbow and compared the handwriting on my tattoo to the book.

It was a match.

I clutched it to my chest for a moment. Tucker was watching me.

"And here is the laptop." He moved it under the table.

I didn't want that. I wanted the book.

"Where can I go to look at this by myself?" I asked.

"Anywhere you want." Still, he didn't move. Neither did my father's legs or shoes.

"I want to come out." My back was hurting a lot.

"Okay." Tucker scooted backward. "But I wish you'd look at the video first."

I crawled out from under the table, clutching my book. "No."

He glanced at my father.

"Did you fix things?" my father asked.

"No," Tucker said. "I couldn't take anything out. It's what her mother used to do. I never want to be like her."

"Mom is bad," I said. "I have the tattoo."

The two of them glanced at each other again.

No more. No more. I raced from the room and realized there was another way out of the hall with the pictures. It led to another small hall with three doors.

I dashed into the first one I came to. It was a bathroom. Perfect. I slammed the door and stood with my back against it so I would know if anyone tried to come in.

This room was blue and white. It took a moment to identify everything by name, as if my brain was only slowly finding words. Shower curtain, toilet, rug, sink, mirror.

Mirror.

I stepped away from the door and set the book on the small counter. I didn't look like any of the versions of myself I'd seen so far. In Vinnie's video, my hair was shorter than in the photos on the wall.

Here, my hair was everywhere. Some of it was stuck to the side of my head with sparkling combs. Other parts fell to my shoulders in thick coils.

I pulled on one of the spirals to make it straight. When I let go, it bounced back into place.

The combs didn't come out easily, caught in tiny strands of hair. I jerked them out and left them on the counter. I opened a few drawers, finding hairbrushes, combs, and tubes and bottles of all sizes.

I could read the labels, but I wasn't sure what some of them meant. Lubriderm. Colgate. Burt's Bees.

I didn't have time to investigate. I picked up my book and sat on the floor with my back against the door. Time to read.

My fingers trembled as I opened it to the first page.

The correct handwriting continued, but my breath caught as my eyes scanned the page.

Mother stole the last book.
   I can't believe it.
   How could she!
   I knew things were missing. I knew it!
   I hate her! I hate her! I hate her!

Here's what I know:

．　．　．

The year is 2017.

You are 17 years old.

You have epilepsy.

At some point (age 6? 7?) the seizures got worse, and you started losing your memory. First, just stupid stuff, like what you had for breakfast. Then bigger stuff, like your last birthday. Holes. Like a Swiss-cheese brain.

Now, you sometimes wake up, and your whole life is wiped clean.

You started keeping a diary when you were nine so you could keep track of things.

You often talked about Mother.

She can't STAND you talking bad about her.

So she STOLE your book.

GOD!

Then she tried to replace it with HER OWN. In HER hand-writing! How much you love her. What a good girl you want to be. BLAH, BLAH, BLAH.

No!

You've hidden notes to yourself. Search hard because she knows you've done it and will find anything easy. The notes will lead you to a book. There will always be a book. It will always have THIS handwriting.

Listen to the voice inside to find it. Something about it stays with you even if you lose your memories. There's a part of you that is always you.

Trust it.

Trust nothing else.

I pressed my hand to my neck. Everything in me shook. Mother was bad. Very bad. I set down the book and stood up, pushing the white sweatpants down to look at the tattoo again.

Mom is bad.

Did I have anything else tattooed on me? There was the warning on my arm, of course. And the name and birthday.

I stripped off the sweatshirt and pants.

Yes. Another one. On my collarbone.

I spun around so my back was to the mirror. Nothing back there.

I examined my belly, my legs, my ankles. I lifted my hair and looked at my neck.

The collarbone one was the only other one.

I leaned into the mirror to see if I could read it.

It was a symbol, the number eight, only sideways.

Infinity. That's what it was. An infinity sign with a small heart.

There were words along the edges. It was hard to make them out in reverse, but I took my time.

The words read, *the heart remembers.*

But I didn't.

Not anything.

I flipped the book open again to a random page.

Men can't be trusted.

I scanned the page. I was living with a bunch of women then. I sounded upset and scared.

This I could relate to.

I flipped to another one.

Taking photos is the best! The words were above several images taped into the book.

At least I sounded happy there. Maybe it wasn't all bad.

Another page had a photo of a long counter. A man

with a heavy beard stood behind it, in front of a huge sign that read, "Big Harry's Diner."

Beneath it, I had written a paragraph.

Big Harry saved you. He owns a diner on South First and gave you a job, helped hide you from your mother, and gave you money for your first college classes. If you are ever in trouble, Big Harry is the one to find.

Huh. Had anyone mentioned Big Harry? This man wasn't at the hospital. Where was he? Would he help me this time? I had no idea where to look.

I closed the cover.

I was so tired.

I wanted to be alone. Lie down. Not think anymore.

CHAPTER 9
Tucker

When Ava emerged from the bathroom, she'd taken her hair down.

Marcus and I stood from the kitchen chairs.

She didn't seem angry or frightened, just tired. I had no idea what she'd read.

When she didn't speak, Marcus said, "We made a plate of food for you. You're probably hungry."

She frowned, clutching the book in front of her. "How do I know if I'm hungry?"

Marcus glanced at me. He had never seen Ava in the first hours after a memory reset. You could take nothing for granted. Even though she might understand a word like hungry and that it meant you should eat, the experience of feeling hungry wouldn't connect until she was taught it.

I needed to take the lead on this. "Your stomach might make noises. You might get a headache. But mainly, when you see food"—I held up a plate with a croissant and some cheese, leftovers from the brunch—"you want it. Bad."

Her eyes focused on the plate. Yeah, she was hungry. I

set the plate on a space I'd cleared and pulled out a chair. "Sit here. Eat."

She did, keeping the book in her lap, her back tall and rigid, like she might bolt at any moment. She picked up a cube of cheddar and popped it into her mouth.

As soon as she chewed, she sank down in the chair, setting the book on the table. "That's so good." She ate several more cubes as fast as she could, then took a bite of the croissant. "So good."

"Does anything hurt?" Marcus asked. "You didn't fall or anything, but do you have any pain?"

She shook her head. "My back hurt when I was under the table, but it doesn't anymore." Crumbs fell out of her mouth as she spoke. Yeah, manners didn't come naturally either. I couldn't help but bite back a smile.

"I'll get you some water," Marcus said.

"Did you get to read some pages?" I asked her.

She swallowed her bite. "A few. I understand why I have the tattoo that mom is bad."

Marcus set the glass in front of Ava. "I still don't think she can be trusted. You stopped going to visit her a couple of years ago when she tried to convince you to stop taking your meds."

Ava's eyes went wide over the rim of the glass as she guzzled water. She started speaking before she'd completely swallowed. "But I only missed one day of meds, and I had a seizure. Why would she say that?"

Marcus rocked on his heels, hands linked behind his back. "She was frustrated with your medicines. She had you on medical marijuana."

Ava's face screwed up in confusion. "I don't understand that."

"It's another type of drug," Marcus said. "It goes in

and out of being illegal depending on where you live. But it's not reliable. There's no quality control. No dosing. It did work, but it's a very risky way to go. The med you're on now worked beautifully until…" he trails off.

"Until I forgot it." Ava stared at her plate. "I understand that I brought this on myself."

"No," I said. "You and I always look out for each other. I should have checked. You had a busy day." And I should have. I should have verified she'd taken them before I left.

Except they were doing makeup in the kitchen. And Ava didn't want me to see her until the ceremony. So, I didn't go in there.

"Your condition isn't your fault," Marcus said. "Sometimes we have to work with the hand we're dealt."

Ava's face screwed up at that.

"It's a reference to a card game," I said. "You can't control the cards that come up in the deck."

"Oh," Ava said. "I get it."

"Expressions like that will come back quickly," I told her. "If you talk to people and watch some television, you start to get the references."

She pushed the plate away. "I'm so tired. Can I lie down for a while before I do anything else?"

"Of course," I said. "I'll give you a tour of the house. I think you should probably take your missed dose, though."

I opened the purple box and set a pill in front of her. "Do you know how to swallow it?"

"Of course." She took the pill easily, unlike one of the times she'd lost her memory when I'd had to teach her.

"Ready?" I glanced at Marcus meaningfully, but he didn't take the hint. And I supposed I understood. One of the times Ava had lost her memory, she'd bolted from me and run to her mother, not knowing that it was a terrible choice.

At least she wouldn't do that this time.

I pointed to the hall. "You already saw the entryway with your photos. And the living room."

She nodded.

"The kitchen is pretty straightforward. You found the bathroom." I left the kitchen.

She got up, leaving the book behind. Marcus looked like he was going to nab it. I'd talk to him about it later.

Ava followed me into the side hall.

I pointed to the front of the house. "Up there is the spare bedroom. You use it as your office for your photography."

"Really?" She walked that way and peered in.

I stood behind her. Huge, mounted portraits were stacked against one wall. A bookcase was filled with flashes, camera mounts, lenses, and photo albums. Her primary workstation computer sat on a desk, silent and dark. Two cameras were tucked under the trio of monitors.

"That's a lot of screens," she said.

"For editing your photos."

She flipped through the images in the stack. Scenes from Austin. Some weddings. Florals. Closeups of turtles and kayaks on the lake.

"It feels good in here," she said.

"It's your favorite space."

She lifted one of the cameras and peered at it. "I don't know how to use this anymore."

"You'll pick it back up. Vinnie can help."

She frowned. "Okay." She set the camera down again.

I caught the change in emotion. "Do you not want Vinnie?"

"I don't know. Do you know who Big Harry is?"

So, she'd read about him. That was good. Harry was someone who always made her feel safe.

"Of course. He was at the wedding."

"Can I see him?"

"Absolutely. I'll call him over."

She took in the rest of the room, turning in a circle. "Can I sleep first? I'm really tired."

"Yes, let me show you the bedroom."

I led her down the hall. Entering our space was way harder than I expected. Only hours before, we had been lying in this bed together, excited about our wedding day.

Now, she didn't know me.

"A bed," she said, falling on top of the blanket. "It smells so good."

"Your favorite fabric softener."

She snuggled in. She had automatically chosen her side. "Is everyone going to leave?"

"We want to make sure you're safe."

"I need some time to myself."

My throat tightened. "Of course. I'll close the door. I'll be in the living room if you need me."

Her eyes were drifting closed before I could even make it to the hall. Post-ictal. It was a tough state, right after a seizure. I'd been through it plenty.

Marcus waited by the kitchen door, the scrapbook in his hand. "Is she resting?"

"Yeah. She's going to need to sleep this off."

"Can she get out through the bedroom window?"

I understood his concern. Ava ran before. "I don't think that will happen."

"I think we should edit the book," he said. "And see

about removing that tattoo. It's doing more harm than good."

"One thing at a time," I told him. Standing up to Marcus was difficult. He had money, age, and a powerful position.

And I still wasn't Ava's husband.

"I won't have a repeat of 2018," he said.

"Then do a stakeout," I told him. "I'm going to let her sleep." I held out my hand for the book.

He stared at it for a moment, then reluctantly passed it to me.

"While she's sleeping, I'll put sticky notes throughout it. I'll explain things. Mitigate any damage. She's already asked for Harry, though."

Marcus sat on one of the kitchen chairs again, seeming defeated. "She always chooses him."

"He's good for her."

Marcus fiddled with the corner of one of the boxes piled on the table. "He is. I guess I just wish she preferred me."

I knew exactly how he felt, but I wouldn't say it.

I tucked the book under my arm. "I'm going to get on this so it's ready when she wakes."

Then I left him behind in the kitchen, the scene of the crime where the meds had been missed, the schedule had changed, and my life—all our lives—had been completely upended.

CHAPTER 10

Ava

When I woke up, everything was dark.

I sat up, alarm bells clanging inside my head.

At least I was alone. I understood that Tucker lived here, too, but he hadn't tried to crawl into bed beside me. I'd seen all the rooms in this house. There was only one bed anywhere.

The clock read 9:46. I couldn't remember when I had lain down.

I needed more of the medicine they had given me in the hospital. Every movement made my head ache so hard that I felt dizzy.

A line of light seeped in from under the door, so I walked carefully toward it, my arms outstretched in case I bumped into something.

I felt around for the knob and opened it.

It creaked more loudly than I liked, and I held my breath, listening. Could I really be alone now? Maybe Tucker and my father had gone to the wedding after all, like they'd asked the others to do at the hospital.

I took a few steps down the hall. When I neared the

bathroom, a powerful pinching sensation came over me low, below my belly. What was that?

I pressed my hands against my stomach. Was I sick?

Tucker appeared from the direction of the living room. He still wore the suit pants and shirt but had taken off the shiny shoes. "I thought I heard you. You okay?"

Not alone after all. It might be for the best because I understood nothing. "My head hurts," I told him. "And something in my stomach. It makes me feel anxious, like I should jump up and down."

He glanced at the bathroom. "You might need to go to the bathroom." He gestured to the door. "Do you know what to do in there?"

I thought about it, searching for what I had done there before. Looked at the book. Looked in the mirror. There was a shower. That was for washing, like the sink.

And the toilet. "I sit on the toilet. And that makes this feeling go away, right?" It all felt very abstract, like I knew the information, but I couldn't imagine what it was like to do it.

"That's right. Your body will know what to do once you lower your clothes and sit down. The toilet paper is there to clean up." His face began shifting in color, darker and redder. "Do you want me to help?"

No, no, I did not. I dashed into the room and closed the door.

Now that I was inside, the urgency grew stronger. I examined the toilet. There seemed to be several parts. I lifted the lid. There was a circle opening.

I assumed I sat on that. I needed instructions. But I pulled down my pants and sat down, realizing too late that the underwear should go, too. Water streamed out of me, soaking the panties.

Of course, they both had to go. Why hadn't I done that?

I kicked off the sweatpants, trying to avoid getting them wet. Then I slid the panties down. This was a disaster.

I tossed the panties into the sink and dried myself off with toilet paper. Now, what? I ran clean water over the panties. They were really wet. I left them in the sink.

I dried my hands and put the sweatpants back on. It felt strange to wear them without underwear, but I couldn't do anything about it. There were probably other panties somewhere in the bedroom.

When I went back to the hall, Tucker was still there. "Uh, Harry is here. We had him come in case you woke up."

"Really?" I could conjure the image of him since I'd seen the picture in the book.

"Come on." He walked through the hall with the pictures to the room with the sofa.

Harry sat on the blue cushions, which were smashed beneath his weight. He was so much bigger than Tucker, his legs stretched out in front of him in a blue suit. He had a massive dark beard and so much hair on his head. You could see only his eyes and nose.

But he looked like his picture, and the smile he gave was so big that you could suddenly make out his mouth in all that hair.

"Ava, my girl! I heard you asked for me, and ol' Harry isn't ever going to wait a second when my Ava calls for me."

He stood and strode right up to me, hauling me into his arms.

At first, I stiffened. I'd avoided anyone touching me if I

could help it, but there was something different about Harry. He was so big and cuddly and smelled exactly right.

I melted against his huge frame, and before I could stop it, I was crying, crying so hard my whole body shook.

"That's all right, sweet Ava. Let it out." He sat down again, drawing me against his side, his hand on my hair.

I cried and cried and couldn't seem to stop. Harry held on to me, squeezing my shoulders, making a "Shhh, shhh" sound until I started hiccupping.

"Can you get my girl some water?" Harry asked.

Footsteps receded. Tucker's, I guess.

"We took care of everything," Harry said. "Everybody had dinner, and Tucker's Gram made all the announcements. We brought some of the food back for you."

I pulled back to look up at him. "Is anyone else here?"

"Just me and Tucker. Your father will be back in the morning. He went to help with the wedding issues. People to pay and all that."

"Oh, I guess it still cost money even though we didn't get married."

"Don't you worry a hair on your head about that, sweet girl."

"I don't want anyone here. Except maybe you."

Harry nodded. "I understand. It's bound to be bewildering. But you need someone to look after you while you get your bearings. It's a big, wild world out there, and you have a lot to learn again."

I knew he was right. "But it's hard with…" I trailed off when Tucker returned.

"Ah, I see," Harry said. He took the glass from Tucker. "My good boy, what does Ava need to see her through until morning?"

Tucker's lips pressed together. "She'll probably be hungry again. And she will need something for her headache. And she won't know how to work anything in the house, like the microwave or maybe even locks."

"Show us where the meds are. I can handle the food." Harry stood up.

"What are you saying?" Tucker asked.

"I'm saying, let's give Ava a moment. Why don't you go fetch your Gram and stay the night with her? I'll handle Ava tonight. We can talk about her life and look at pictures if she likes. I think I know as much as anybody about where she's been."

Tucker's face had gone dark again. "But I need to show her the videos. Get her reoriented."

"I hear you. I agree. I'm saying tomorrow is as good as any. The girl needs to feel safe, and right now, that's the big thing. I know you're worried about the time I took her to her mother, but I'm in the know now, and she'll be right safe with me."

Tucker looked at me. I didn't have anything to say, but he must have figured out something from how I looked. "Okay. But keep me updated." He bent down to push my book to me across a short table in front of us. "I put some notes in your book to explain some things that might be alarming. If you want to look at any videos, the laptop is here. I turned the password off, so you can simply open it and hit play." He straightened, still frowning. "I'll come back tomorrow."

"That's a good lad," Harry said. "I think she'll be better without so much going on around her. We'll have a good chat."

Tucker turned to me. "I don't want to leave," he said.

"But I will if that's what you want. I'll always do what you want."

A rush of competing emotions flooded my system, making me feel so much worse than I had when I woke up. I pressed my hand to my chest, then to my head, and closed my eyes.

"You sit here, Ava, and take long, slow breaths," Harry said. "I'll have Tucker show me a few things, and then we'll have him run along."

He got up from the sofa. I curled against the cushioned arm, breathing like Harry told me to.

I understood who Tucker was supposed to be to me. And my father, too. But my own words told me who Harry was. And he was the one who made me feel at home.

Until I could handle all the ways everyone made me feel, I needed to take this life one moment, and one person, at a time.

CHAPTER 11

Tucker

Gram sat across from me at the breakfast table, where we'd shared a lot of meals before I finally got to move in with Ava two years ago.

Her hands circled her coffee cup, nails painted pink for the wedding. "What will you do about the honeymoon?"

Right, Ava and I were scheduled to leave for Alaska this afternoon. She had been so excited to photograph whales and sharks and glaciers.

"She won't go. I won't even suggest it. She only wants Harry."

Gram stared into her cup. "I can't believe it happened yesterday of all days."

"No, it makes sense that it did. She was off schedule. Out of the norm. Extra stressed." I ran a finger around the rim of the cup.

"Have you heard from Harry this morning?"

"Yeah. He said she finally went to bed around three. That the two of them went through a few pages of the book and read my sticky notes."

"Did she watch any of the videos?"

"No. She only trusts the book and handwriting. Marcus wants us to have her tattoo removed so she won't keep going back to that."

Gram set down her mug with a soft clunk. "You think the book will help?"

"I don't know. It never seems to."

We fell quiet. I tried not to despair over having to spend what should have been my wedding night in the bed I'd slept in for thirteen years after I'd arrived following my family's accident.

My head buzzed again, like it had in the car at the hospital. This time, I had my magnet in my pocket, so I pulled it out and passed it over the device in my chest to add an extra electrical zap, just in case.

Gram watched me, her gray eyebrows furrowed. "How often do you have to do that?"

"Rarely. But the stress might be getting to me, too."

She stood and picked up our plates of scrambled eggs and toast. Neither of us had eaten much. "Do you tell your doctor when you have to manually set it off?"

I shrugged. "No. Not unless something breaks through. And it hasn't."

The dishes rattled in the sink. "Do you think Ava will see you today?"

I had no idea. Ava hadn't been using her phone. I texted her a few times, careful, easy things, asking her how she was. She'd have to relearn how to use it. Knowledge like that never stuck. Harry wouldn't prioritize it.

"I'll go over there later. Knock on my own door, I guess."

Gram turned on the water, passing her hand beneath it occasionally to check the temperature. "You can stay here as long as you need."

I was hoping I wouldn't have to, but the way this reset was going, I might not have a choice. Ava always emerged fearful and untrusting, except with Harry. Maya, too. They'd known her for a long time, Maya the longest. She was her neighbor from her early teens.

Harry had given her a job when she'd lived in a women's shelter, a position that had allowed her to get an apartment and live on her own. He'd protected her since she was eighteen, even from me, at first.

I had to rely on him to guide her back to me, at least in these early days.

Marcus must have gone down the same mental rabbit holes because he texted me a few minutes later.

Marcus: I assume I should cancel the flights and excursions in Alaska?

He was staying at a hotel near the country club, where Ava and I were supposed to be as well.

Me: Yes. She asked me to leave. Harry is with her.

Marcus: I planned to stop by again before heading back to Houston. Or I can stay and send Tina on with the girls.

I understood why he might want to push. We all had to reestablish who we were.

Me: Maybe go see her and then decide. Let me know when you go so we don't overwhelm her with too many visitors.

Marcus: We're about to check out here. I'll go there first and see how she is. I'll report back.

I set down my phone. I was grateful that Marcus always included me. He could have tried to take Ava with him, set her up with doctors in Houston, three hours away. But he always respected our relationship, even when it was completely one-sided, like now.

Gram finished washing the dishes, and I hadn't helped. I stood to dry them, but she motioned me back down.

"Let me dote on you for today. You've earned it. Was that Marcus texting you?"

"Yeah. He's handling the honeymoon. I hate how much money he's out with all this."

Gram sat opposite me again. "It was a lovely dinner. Everyone was so sad for both of you. There were many toasts that Ava would come around quickly, and we'd get to gather again for vows."

"I don't even know what sort of wedding we'll attempt next time."

"Something simpler, I'd assume."

"Definitely."

"Why don't you put together some photos from your phone and have them printed out? If Ava wants her book, create more pages for it. Do it now while things are hard, and you're motivated. That way, it's done in case, God forbid, anything happens again."

She was right. "That's a good idea." I couldn't necessarily access the files that were stored on the computer at home, but I had my phone on me, and much of our relationship was documented there.

She stood up and headed to her room. "I'll put together a grocery list since it seems like you'll be here a few days. I don't think I can get by with a full-grown man on tuna fish and cucumber salads."

"I'll pick it all up when I have the photos printed."

"It'll be all right, Tucker. You've been fighting this battle for going on eight years, and you'll fight it until the end."

I sat at her table, thumbing through photos of Ava and me, the most recent ones first. The last two years had been so easy. Planting the flowers at our house. Setting up her home office. Moving in new furniture. Getting the keys to the house together.

Dinners out. Kayaking on Lady Bird Lake. Dinners at Big Harry's Diner.

Then back to the last reset. We'd videoed some of that on our phones. I had her meeting Maya again, sitting among the flowers on her porch.

Hugging Big Harry, looking exactly like she had last night, lost in his enormous chest.

And before that loss. Sitting among her photographs. Learning to drive again.

So many moments lost to her. Left with me.

I had promised to be the keeper of her memories, and I wouldn't waver now.

This was the time she needed me the most.

CHAPTER 12

Ava

The week following the wedding went slowly. Every day, I spent an hour or so with Tucker, looking at pictures and videos. Then, an hour with Vinnie, trying to figure out my camera and photo software.

But being with Harry was when I felt the safest. I knew he was ignoring his restaurant for me, so when another boring week had passed, I asked him to let me work there so I could do something with myself.

Big Harry's turned out to feel more like home to me than the blue house. It smelled right, like fried food and beer. It was busy, and I liked seeing people for only a short while. With the variety of experiences, accents, and personalities in the diner, I was learning fast.

But today, I had trouble.

Big Harry told me to try to handle it, and he'd step in if he was needed. I liked that. He trusted me to figure things out, unlike Vinnie and Tucker and my dad, who all acted like I was made of glass.

I closed the cash drawer with a bump of my hip, dodged a bar back who was refilling the ice trough, and steeled myself to confront the four middle-aged men laughing at a table near the jukebox. The song playing was "All My Exes Live in Texas," which was probably their doing.

I could totally believe they were up to their eyeballs in exes.

"You forgot one of the tickets," I told them, slamming their pile of cash and printouts onto the middle of the table. "You gotta pay all four."

A man with a bushy beard sat back in his seat, revealing a huge belly with the words, "My kid beat up your honor student," stretched over it on a faded T-shirt.

Classy.

He sniffed before saying, "Now, little lady, it's not our fault if we asked for three checks, and you brought four. We paid the three we said we would."

They *had* asked for three, with two of them on one ticket. And I had messed it up. But still, I wasn't born *yesterday*. Not quite.

"So, obviously you pay two of them together. Where is the unpaid check?" I stood firm, aiming the fiercest stare I could manage.

Maybe I'd seen these scumbags before in my life, maybe I hadn't. They could have been regulars from way back.

But this crew hadn't been in Big Harry's Diner since my memory reset. I had too little rattling around in my head to miss that.

I also had deep abiding knowledge of every episode of *Schitt's Creek* I'd seen in the last week. That and Harry's battle documentaries were the only TV shows I'd watched so far, so I had room to store all the details.

Including David Rose's stare of doom.

Which now was mine.

Another man snorted. "Seems like it got lost, sugar pie. Guess you'll have to take it out of your tip."

As if the paltry three dollars extra they'd thrown in would cover the double chicken-fried steak and two beers.

"I'll reprint it, then," I said.

"We're on our way out," the first man said, standing up to hitch his jeans back into place. "Gotta get back to that demo job." He shoved a yellow hard hat on his head to cover his bald spot.

The other men followed suit in a squeal of table legs on the concrete floor.

I was not getting shorted. Not today. Time to call in my backup.

"Harry!" I called. "We got walkers!"

The first time I heard the term, I thought my coworker literally meant people who could walk. But a couple of days into waiting tables here, Big Harry explained it meant someone who was trying to walk the check, or leave without paying.

Maybe the ground didn't exactly shake as Big Harry lumbered out of his office beyond the bar, but I bet it could have if he'd stomped much harder.

Big Harry had owned this diner for thirty years, right in this spot on South First, and nobody messed with him. He'd once tossed an entire football team out on their butts when they'd gotten too friendly with one of his servers.

My coworkers loved telling me all the Harry stories I'd forgotten.

"Stop right there, or I'll break a leg on each of ya," he bellowed at the men, who were halfway to the door.

They glanced over their shoulders. The last two sped up, but the first one stopped, and they smashed together like the accordion a man had brought in on my first day when he'd played a few songs for tips. Harry let people do that sometimes, particularly if they seemed down on their luck.

Joseph, one of the other servers, raced to the door and locked the deadbolt that used a key on both sides.

No way out.

The lunch crowd quieted. Most of them were regulars and enjoyed a good Harry show. A couple of them hid smiles behind their hands.

I waited by the table, my fists on my hips. "It was another fourteen dollars, if memory serves." My memory didn't serve me whatsoever, but I knew my numbers.

The man in the honor student T-shirt fished out his wallet and flung a twenty-dollar bill in my direction. It fluttered through the air, landing on another table. A young guy, all red hair and freckles, picked it up and passed it to a woman at the next table, and she handed it to me.

Joseph silently returned to the door and unlocked it.

"Out with ya," Harry roared. "And I don't need the likes of you in my establishment ever again."

The one who tossed the twenty looked like he wanted to clap back at that, but he thought better of it and pushed through the door.

When the four of them had taken off down the bright sidewalk awash with afternoon heat, the other customers cheered.

I stuffed the money and tickets in my apron pocket and stacked their plates. The fourth ticket was stuck to the bottom of a cup using congealed gravy as the glue. Jerks.

Harry patted my shoulder. "There'll always be a few of

those. The good people outnumber them all." He gestured to the other tables. "Don't worry. You did right fine."

I piled silverware and napkins onto the plates. "How did I used to handle customers like them? You know, in the time before."

"A little tougher than today. But when you first arrived, no more than a wee mite of eighteen, you were as skittish as a dragonfly."

"So, I got better." I hefted the stack of dishes to take to the back.

"You did." Harry grinned at me, and all the anxiety in my belly over the encounter evaporated. I knew I should think of my actual dad as my dad, but it was Harry who understood me best.

I pushed through the swinging door to the kitchen.

I also knew from my notes that Tucker was a good one. And he'd been very patient, moving back in with his Gram to only visit each day to try to get me back into my old life.

But sometimes I wasn't sure I wanted to.

My tattoos warned me that my life was not always safe. I glanced at the one on my wrist for the thousandth time.

Trust only this handwriting.

CHAPTER 13

Tucker

I was still pretty much in hell.

I sat on Gram's flowered sofa, waiting for her to get dressed so we could head to Big Harry's Diner to see Ava, if only for an hour while we ate.

Before she started working, I got to see her every day. But now that I was back at Jiffy Lube, and she was at Harry's, I didn't always get a chance to go over to our blue house when she was there.

I wasn't making much headway. Our time together felt like two classmates studying the same material, not two people who almost got married finding their way back to each other.

Gram came out of her bedroom in a bright yellow dress with red flowers. Her gray curls looked like they hadn't been colored in yet compared to the outfit.

"Ava liked this one," Gram said. "Did you choose wisely? We should do everything we can to help your cause."

"Yeah." I was actually wearing the same thing I'd worn when I'd met her eight years ago, my dad's bowling shirt.

Gram's face softened as she looked over the green and white shirt. "I remember the day your father bought those shirts. Did you know he asked me what to do back then when he only seemed to connect with your little brother?"

I didn't. "What did he say?"

She sat next to me, resting her big gray purse on her lap. "He noticed you didn't want to throw the ball around like Stephen did, and you preferred to play video games."

"I remember."

"And he asked me what he should do."

"What did you tell him?"

"First, I told him to talk to your mother! Nobody wants a meddling mother-in-law." She said it with such energy that I had to laugh.

"But you had the answer, I take it."

"She got your dad to play some games with you. And that was good. But Stephen wasn't good at those. He needed something all three of you could do."

"So, you suggested bowling."

"I did. Your grandfather and I were in a league back in our day. Of course, bowling in the late sixties often meant doing it either drunk or high."

"Gram!"

She patted my knee. "Oh, you sweet children of today, assuming the old people were always dull. Are you ready?"

I nodded. As we headed for the door, I spotted the last family portrait I'd taken with Mom and Dad and Stephen. I was twelve, Stephen ten. Dad stood tall and athletic. Mom was spindly, like me, but with a big smile in red lipstick.

The accident couldn't have been too long after we'd taken that. In the photo, I was wearing the same red shirt

I'd had on that terrible day when they'd covered my family in plastic.

I could still see the whir of the colored lights. The sheen of rain coming down.

Gram pulled on the front door. It tended to stick, so I rushed up behind her to help.

"Thank you, Tucker." We headed out into the sunshine to her old Buick. "I think this will be the day Ava turns things around."

I wasn't sure why she felt that today would be any different. But I had to hold on to hope. Life had already taken from me more than I could bear. I would not lose Ava, not now, not ever.

When we arrived at the old diner, Gram took my arm as we stepped onto the curb. "Don't fret, Tucker. Show her your good side. She'll come around."

"It's been so slow going this time. She only trusts Harry."

"Thank God for Harry, though. She didn't run."

"True. At least she didn't run."

I opened the diner's door to a rush of refrigerated air. Harry liked his restaurant cold. I waited for Gram to go inside, then drew in a deep breath to steel myself.

Seeing Ava was hard to face. Where she'd once lit up when I entered a room, now she put up an emotional wall. I could see it every time, those bricks dropping into place.

Big Harry sat at the bar at the back of the diner. He lifted his hand in greeting. "Ava's got the booths on the right side today."

I nodded and headed for an empty one, my hand on Gram's arm.

Ava was writing an order for a gray-haired couple. There were only a few tables taken. That was why we'd chosen this time to come. It would be easier to talk to her than when the restaurant was busy.

Gram sat on one side of the booth, and I took the other. Ava scribbled her notes, and I waited for her to look up and notice us. I always watched for any shift in her feelings toward me.

Watching her easy conversation with the older couple made my chest pang. No matter how Ava came out of a memory-erasing seizure, there were things about her that never changed.

The way she spun her hair on her finger. How she bent forward when she was trying to listen, her head tilted slightly to the left.

"I'll get this put in," Ava said to the other table, straightening as she turned away. She spotted us at our booth, and there it was. *Slam.* The wall came down.

"I'll be right back," she said in our direction, then headed to the kitchen.

Harry watched her go, then said to us, "Rough lunch hour. She's got her tail over her back."

Great. It was even harder to connect with her when she was already out of sorts.

"Stay the course, Tucker," Gram said. "It's worth it."

She was right. And I never doubted that. I just wished life were easier for us.

Ava emerged from the kitchen, looking resigned to waiting on us.

"Hello, dear," Gram said. "It's lovely to see you."

"And you," Ava said. "Hello, Tucker."

My throat constricted. Her hair was twisted up in pinwheels like it had been years ago. She must have seen a picture of herself with them and liked it.

"I like your 'do."

Her head tilted. "My do?"

"Hairdo. Sorry. I forget idioms don't automatically come back."

She frowned. I'd reminded her of her condition. This never went well. Stupid mistake. I knew better.

"What can I get you today?" she asked.

She was going to stick to all business.

"Well," Gram said. "What I want is a chicken-fried steak drowning in gravy, but if my doctor finds out, he'll have a heart attack on my behalf."

Ava cracked a small smile. "So, a salad, then?"

"I suppose so."

"How about I mix in some grilled chicken and some fried chicken strips so you are a little bit healthy and a little bit naughty?"

Gram set down her menu. "I like the way you think."

A pang of jealousy zipped through my chest. It was so easy for Gram to connect with Ava. I always did everything wrong.

"You know what you want?" Ava asked me. I didn't miss the guardedness in her tone.

"A cheeseburger."

"Got it." She collected the menus. "And water?"

We both nodded.

Then, she was gone.

"That went well," Gram said.

I stared at the scarred wooden tabletop. "Sure, if you were placing an order and not trying to convince her to give you the time of day."

"You'll get there."

Gram was right. But in the last pinwheel hair era, Ava had read all her notes and still rejected me. It had taken months to make inroads then.

But now we had a house together, a situation to figure out. This created added pressure for both of us. I wanted things back to where we had been. She wanted to live her new life.

It was unbearable.

We fell silent as Ava returned with the water. I expected her to dart away again, but she paused.

"I found a couple of shirts that are too big for me. I think you missed them when you packed."

"Which ones?"

"An AC/DC that says 'Highway to Hell.' And a red one with the Shelfmart logo."

I knew what she was talking about. "You stole the AC/DC one from me because that was the song playing when we met. You liked to wear it to—" I cut myself off before I said, "Bed." "You liked to wear it. And the Shelfmart one was always yours. They gave you the wrong size when you first worked there."

"I worked at Shelfmart?"

"Yes, when you escaped your mother."

This got her attention. "Wait? I had to *escape* my mother?"

So, she definitely had never finished all the videos or even her own stories written out. If she had, she would have known.

"When you were eighteen. She lied to you after a memory reset and told you that you were sixteen so you wouldn't run away."

"More juice behind the ol' tattoo." She looked down at her thigh as if she could see *Mom is bad* through her jeans. "Why don't I have a tattoo about you?"

"You do."

"I don't have the name Tucker anywhere on my body."

Gram stood up. "If you'll excuse an old lady with a weak bladder, I'll be back in a moment."

Gram was good like that. When she was gone, I turned to Ava. "We got matching ones. We thought it would be enough."

"My birth date?"

"No, the symbol." I pulled down the collar of my shirt to reveal the infinity sign with the words, "The heart remembers."

"Oh," she said, frowning. She certainly frowned a lot when I was around. "I do have that one." She let out a long, slow breath. "My dad said I should let you move back in. So has Harry."

My heart sped up. "Will you?"

"I can't. I just can't. You get that, right? I barely know who I am. How am I supposed to add you to the mix?"

I understood. I did. And it wasn't the first time she'd said this to me.

"I get it. But maybe we could go out? On a date?"

She pressed her lips together, tapping the table with her finger. "Maybe."

My body washed over with hope. "Okay." I had to be careful here. "Maybe in a few days? Which night do you have off?"

"Tomorrow."

I forced the quaver out of my voice as I said, "I'll come over tomorrow."

"Fine. Tomorrow. But no more of the home videos. Something else."

"Totally. Anything you want to do. Maybe a movie. Or a restaurant other than Harry's?"

"All right." She took off to check on the other couple.

The words rang in my mind as I waited for Gram to return.

All right.

She'd said, *All right.* To a date.

For the first time since I'd lost her, I felt hope.

CHAPTER 14

Ava

Well, that was done. I'd agreed to go on a date with Tucker.

The matching tattoos had me shook. Why had I done that? I understood the ones with warnings. And of course, the tattoo with my name and birthdate. Essential with my condition.

But to get one with this man? I was twenty-five. If you asked Marta, the forty-something server here who'd worked for Harry forever, she'd say you didn't know a damn thing about nothing until you were thirty, much less who to partner up with.

That went double for me. Triple, really.

I brought Tucker and Gram their food and said little else until they left. The older couple were still in a booth, but otherwise, the diner was totally dead.

I wandered among the tables. The gap between my memory and my age was most acute when the diner was quiet. Without the bustle of taking orders, moving from one customer to the next, my head felt empty. Thoughts rattled around like two coins in a tip jar.

I leaned against the counter at the bar, a dish towel tucked in my waistband. Most of the time, all I felt was the need to be alone. To keep my distance. Everyone came at me too fast, even the customers. "Fine weather we're having," one would say.

How did I know? Every day had been more or less the same as long as I'd been alive, mid-nineties and miserable.

Other people had so much to say, so many opinions to make. They got blustery and defensive and wanted you to agree with them.

I just wanted to learn what I needed to survive. I saw the envelopes that had arrived at the house. Water bill. Electric. Cell phones. I needed money to pay them. I had to work, and the camera was hard. Vinnie had finished all the orders that needed to go out. We'd slowed down before my wedding, so that was another saving grace.

I told Vinnie to take all the clients booked out and hire his own second shooter. He wanted me to try it, sure I would pick it up quickly, but it was too stressful. I didn't want it. Not yet.

Big Harry's was easy.

I wiped down the bar, not that it needed it. Happy hour hadn't begun yet. Anyone who stopped in for lunch had already stumbled out, other than that one couple who sat across from each other, taking their time sharing a slice of lemon meringue pie.

I kept glancing in their direction because the quiet joy radiating from their table was brighter than the St. Pauli Girl sign blinking over their heads.

The old man held one of the woman's hands clasped between both of his. His eyes sparkled as he looked at her. I could only see half of her face, but based on her forward lean and the flirting smile, she felt the same way about him.

She wore a simple gold band on her left hand, and I figured they'd been married forever. I wandered behind the bar and shoved a metal scoop into the ice trough to break up the big chunks, trying to guess their story. Did they meet when she was a girl of sixteen and he a young man about to head off to Vietnam? World War II?

I didn't know my dates very well. In fact, I only knew those wars existed because Harry had watched a zillion documentaries during the week he stayed with me. The history of the world had been zapped from my memory right along with my own personal story. But I was learning.

The man lifted the woman's hand to kiss her fingers. He must have known what got to her because her cheeks turned pink. What was that like? To have someone know you so well?

Did Tucker know me that well? Had we been like that couple?

A buzz zipped through my body at the thought of it. What was that? I pressed my hand to my belly, paying attention to the feeling. Was it making me sick?

I didn't think so. It was thrilling, like when I first got in the gray car in the driveway that opened with one of the keys on my ring. My hands knew what to do when I sat in the seat. The engine chugged to life, and my fingers automatically closed around the knob on the stick next to my leg.

It took a minute to work out which direction to go, but my feet figured it out before my brain did, hitting the pedals to make the car move or stop. I only drove around the block once because my doctor said I'd lost my license for three months to make sure there wouldn't be another seizure, but it was exciting and wild to have that hunk of metal under my control.

Thankfully, Big Harry's wasn't too far away to walk to.

But this buzz. It was like that one.

I wonder what about Tucker made me feel that way?

I turned away from the couple to the wall of bottles behind the bar and said his name, just to try it. "Tucker."

My arms broke out in goosebumps, and I shivered.

Yeah, he was definitely someone my body knew.

Big Harry came out of his office with the bank bag. "I'm off to make a deposit," he said. "You and Joe got it handled?"

Joseph was in the back flirting with the line cook. "We got it."

He hesitated, and I already figured he was about to say something about Tucker.

But he shook his head and walked on out into the afternoon.

Good.

So many lectures. So much advice. I tried to sort it all out. I figured other people had experiences that helped them understand what was being said.

One thing I saw a lot was moms correcting their kids when they said something mean. They liked to tell Big Harry he was scary or that the food was gross.

The moms would say, "Be polite."

My impulse was to smash a plate of food against their face. I had no idea where that feeling came from. I hadn't seen a single person do that since I'd been alive. It couldn't be common. But I always had to resist, like when those men tried to walk the check. I'd really wanted to lift that plate and smear gravy across their ugly mugs.

But I hadn't.

Be polite.

I hadn't done that either, but they had paid. Harry had set them straight.

Other advice took some time to work out.

Flo, who worked last night, kept saying, "Don't give them an inch, honey, or they'll take a mile."

It took some thinking to figure out what she meant. It had nothing to do with measurement. It meant that if I let a customer get away with a small thing, like touching my hand, then they'd do something bigger, like pinch my butt.

Instinct had taken over on that one, and I'd punched the guy in the nose. He'd stood up in a hurry and backed away.

Harry had handled him, too.

Maybe the only real advice I needed to follow was, "Always have a Harry."

But Harry was only a help at the diner. My life included a lot of other things. Like shopping at Shelfmart for groceries. And figuring out how to work the stove and the washing machine and how to program the air conditioning. I was hopeless with my cell phone, barely able to make a call, much less understand all the colorful icons and what they could do.

I'd have to forge a new path. It might not look like the old Ava's life. It might not include all the same people.

Maybe.

My hand flattened against my chest, pressing against the long bone that ran from my neck to my shoulder. The tattoo was right there.

The heart remembers.

CHAPTER 15

Tucker

Just one more hour of work until I could go clean up and see Ava.

I jumped down into the pit below a 1964 Ford Mustang. It wasn't often we got cars like this in the shop for an oil change. People who bought classics tended to do the maintenance themselves.

I set up a funnel for the drip and unscrewed the drain on the oil pan. Right as the oil started flowing, I heard a long, low whistle from up above.

Feet appeared at the edge of the pit. I knew from the scuffed black-and-white checkered Vans that it was Fuentes.

I walked over and peered up. He was admiring the ride, running a hand over the dark blue paint.

"Don't fingerprint the wax job," I told him with a laugh. "The dude who brought this in is probably going to inspect it from bumper to hood ornament."

Fuentes stepped back, whistling again. "Don't tell me it's some insufferable tech bro who got it for his Tinder pics."

93

"Probably." The oil slowed to a trickle, so I turned back to wait it out, then screwed in the drain plug and wiped away the dribble.

I ran up the steps two at a time to stand next to Fuentes, who had requested that the patch on his Jiffy Lube uniform read, "Short King."

Renee, the office manager who ordered the patches, had tried to helpfully translate it to "Chaparro," and Fuentes had about flipped, insisting that was not what he was going for.

Despite quite a few of the employees having fun nicknames on their patches, mine was plain old "Tucker." I didn't have the humor or the imagination to come up with something clever, particularly when I'd first started, which was right after Ava and I had gotten the blue house.

I hoped one day I'd be back in it.

Fuentes could read my frown any day and asked, "The old lady still not letting you back home?"

"She's having a tougher time this round."

Fuentes nodded thoughtfully, looking over the car. Marcus had told me Fuentes got roaring drunk at the wedding and hit on Ava's college-age sister. Marcus had kicked him out.

Probably, if Ava and I got another wedding, I wouldn't be able to make him a groomsman.

I walked to the engine and twisted the oil filter off. The motor was pristine, as if someone had pressure-washed it.

Fuentes leaned in. "Not original parts. Too bad."

This made the car significantly less interesting. I passed him the dead filter and screwed in the new one.

He set it on the cart. "Gotta be rough, going from banging to banished."

Fuentes was the only one willing to say it. Probably his

bluntness made him a good friend. But a terrible groomsman.

When I didn't reply, Fuentes walked the perimeter of the Mustang, admiring the glossy finish.

Our boss, Domingo, entered the garage space, wiping his hands on a shop towel. "How many of y'all does it take to do an oil change?" he asked.

"I'm going," Fuentes said, heading to the Ford SUV in his bay. His car was a lot less interesting.

Domingo admired the 'stang. "They don't make them like this anymore."

"Might be a good thing," I said, grunting to remove the oil cap. Whoever had changed the oil last time had grossly over-tightened it. "They overheat, and the crappy gas mileage makes driving it require a second job."

Domingo chuckled. "True, but wait until we start it up."

I guessed he was hanging around to listen. I got the cap off and set a funnel in the hole. As I poured in the first quart of oil, we both took in the car like it was a moving picture we couldn't look away from.

"Y'all are in love," Fuentes called from his bay before disappearing below the SUV.

"Might be," Domingo said.

I started my second quart, picturing Ava in the front seat. Right now, we had a gray Honda Accord Ava's dad had given us. But since it came from him, I had left it in the driveway at the house when she'd asked me to leave.

Maybe that wasn't practical since I could drive, and Ava would have to wait at least three months to be cleared again. But I never assumed anything about what our future would bring. Each time was a risk that she wouldn't come back to me.

As I finished the oil change, Domingo settled into the driver's seat. The perks of being the boss.

When the engine roared to life, he cocked his head back, his arm extended to the steering wheel. "Now, this is the life," he called out.

The bays hummed with the perfect timing of the engine. Domingo leaned out the window. "You can go ahead and clock out. I'll handle this."

I wiped my hands on a shop towel. "See you tomorrow."

Time to get to Gram's, shower, and come up with a game plan for tonight. Ava probably needed some help around the house. Had she figured out the trash day yet? When to put out the recycling?

The thermostat might still be in vacation mode. I'd programmed it the morning of the wedding. I should check the air conditioner filter. I hadn't fixed the leaking faucet in the bathroom.

Houses needed maintenance.

Maybe if dating didn't work, that could be how I got near her again.

I'd make a list of chores. A schedule for when I'd come.

Play our old favorite music. Maybe run a movie we liked in the background.

Pop some popcorn. That smell was always happy to her.

I'd figure out a way.

Tonight would be the first real try.

CHAPTER 16

Ava

I wasn't sure what to do to prepare for a date. There weren't very many dates shown on *Schitt's Creek*, and everybody dressed the same. The Rose family was all fancy all the time. The rest of the town was what Flo called Wal-Mart chic, whatever that meant.

I hadn't worked today. I'd spent another long hour with Vinnie and my camera.

Vinnie had been patient in teaching me what I used to know. So far, I had learned about f-stops and apertures and the rule of thirds.

Vinnie said I had an eye for it, and as soon as I understood the settings, I'd be okay again. I wasn't sure.

Since I had a couple of hours before Tucker would come, I wandered the neighborhood with the camera, taking pictures of trees and cars and squirrels when I could spot them. Maybe after I did these by myself, Vinnie could tell me if I still had the eye.

Everyone I passed seemed to know me and smiled and waved. One woman walking a dog called out. "How was the wedding?"

I didn't know what to say. I went with, "It was an eventful day."

I spotted a bright red bird and followed it for a while, hoping to catch it against the sky. I took picture after picture of the bird in a tree, on a wire, on a bush. But every time he flew somewhere, the picture was blurry. I would have to ask Vinnie why.

Eventually, I turned around.

A woman stood in front of the house next door, watering several buckets of flowers by her mailbox. "Hello, Ava," she called. "Taking some pictures?"

"Yeah," I said. "Got some of a red bird." Maybe I could fake this.

"I was telling Ted we sure hadn't seen much of you and Tucker since the wedding! I told him, I bet they're busy being newlyweds!"

Oh. I wondered if I should correct her. But I said, "We are!"

I hurried past. When I turned up the path to the blue house, Tucker was already sitting on the steps. He looked forlorn, staring at his phone, his legs sprawled out in khaki pants ironed with a sharp crease. His shirt had buttons and a collar. Normally, he wore jeans and T-shirts.

Right. The date.

When he spotted me coming up the sidewalk, his face switched to relief. I guessed he thought I was lost or something had happened. "Talking to Isadora?" he asked.

"Is that her name?"

"Yeah. She's lovely. She has a husband named Ted."

"They think we got married. All the neighbors do."

He nodded. "That's okay. It doesn't matter."

"Is it time already?" I asked him.

"Yeah. You don't have your phone?"

"I didn't have any pockets." I walked behind him to pop the front door open.

"You don't lock it?" he asked.

I hesitated. "Should I?"

His jaw tightened, and I could tell he wanted to say more, but he didn't. I guessed maybe I should lock the door. Everyone I met seemed so nice, but maybe there were people nearby who stole things, like the teenagers on *Schitt's Creek* who'd shoplifted in Rose Apothecary. Alexis had called them kleptos.

I couldn't have anyone stealing my book. I needed it.

Tucker followed me inside. "Have you watched any videos since last time?"

"I said no more videos. Besides, I've been working."

Tucker nodded. "Do you have any questions for me?"

Would our date be the same as all the hours we spent going over my old life? I set the camera on the table everyone called a coffee table, which was weird because nobody ever drank coffee there.

But I did have a question for him. "I don't understand the paper flowers." I sat as far from him as possible on the sofa and opened a box I had found.

In it were tons of random things. A coaster from Big Harry's. A pin from Shelfmart that had my name on it. But also, lots and lots of faded colored paper cut in the shape of flowers.

I hadn't read the entire book yet. Focusing on words and figuring out their meaning gave me a headache if I did it for too long. I'd seen references to the paper flowers there and hints that they held all my secrets.

But I couldn't figure out why these old cutouts were important, or where the secrets were.

I pulled out a handful and set them on the table.

Tucker picked one up. "Do you recognize the flower shapes anymore?"

"I think this is a tulip." I pointed to a pink one with points along the top.

"It is." He flattened the one he held in his hand. "This is a rose."

"That's not what the roses on our bushes look like."

He laughed lightly. "Roses look a lot of ways. The tight buds are different from the fully open blooms."

"That's true." I picked up a yellow flower with a long front section. "I have no idea what this is."

This made his smile go away. "That's a daffodil." He swallowed in a way that made his throat bulge for a moment. "We, uh, wow. Okay."

My chest squeezed. I'd said something wrong. "We don't have to talk about it," I said, reaching to gather up the flowers.

He stopped me with a hand resting lightly on mine.

My skin buzzed. I looked at him, wondering what was happening. It was like I was holding the electric toothbrush in my bathroom.

Tucker pulled back. Had he felt it, too? "When we first met at the children's hospital, I told you about my mom. She died with my dad and brother when I was twelve."

"What?" Now it was hard for me to swallow. I pressed my hand to my neck. "Your whole family?"

"Yes, that's why you've never met them. They're not here anymore. We had a car accident, and during that accident, they died, and I got a head injury that caused me to have seizures, like you do."

I moved my hand from my throat to my chest. My heart was thumping so hard, I could feel it in my ears. "I didn't know that."

"We have a lot of ground to cover."

What? "You mean in the yard?"

"No, no. Sorry. It's an expression. I mean there are a lot of things we haven't talked about yet."

This was almost as hard as reading. Understanding random phrases was still difficult. I could see no connection between covering up some ground and talking about his family.

I pointed at the table. "We were talking about the paper flowers."

"Right, right. So, in the hospital, I told you my mother's favorite flowers were daffodils. We painted pictures of them in art therapy, and it kind of became our thing. I brought you a potted daffodil at the duplex where you lived. You started making paper versions for your flower wall. These used to hang in your bedroom."

"But how did they keep my secrets?"

"You were very clever." He picked up the daffodil and turned it over. "See, you would write very small on the backside so it looked like you were making a design on the leaves. But there are words."

I took the daffodil from him and peered at the letters. It read, "Tonight you will tell Tucker you love him."

I set it down abruptly. "I get it." I picked up the pink tulip. On the back of the leaves it said, "Mom stole your journal."

The book said that, too. "Where is Mom now?" I asked everyone this. I wanted to compare Tucker's answer to Dad's and Harry's.

"She still lives out near Wimberley in the house she moved you to back when you were about to turn eighteen. She was trying to get you away from me. She knew if your memory reset, you would forget who I was and not try to leave."

Everyone had mentioned Wimberley, but no one had told me this much. "Did it work?"

"It did." He flipped through the book to pages of densely typed words I hadn't read yet. "The whole story is here. She told you that you were fifteen years old, not eighteen, and kept you away from anyone who might tell you the truth. But then you turned sixteen, according to her. You wanted to get a job since you were old enough, but she wouldn't let you, and you got suspicious and found your birth certificate."

I gripped the edge of the sofa cushion. Mom was indeed bad. "What did I do then?"

"You ran away and got to a librarian who helped you go to a shelter here in Austin."

"I've read notes about the shelter. Men are bad, everyone said."

He nodded. "Yes, there are terrible situations that lead women to go to shelters."

"I saw your sticky note." Tucker had placed one on the page about the shelter. It said, "Some men are bad. Others are good."

"Do you want to read more of the paper flowers?" he asked. "I think you wrote most of them in your usual handwriting at one point." He pointed at the book. "Can I look?"

"Okay."

He flipped through it until he found a page that said, "Paper flowers" at the top. Sure enough, one of the flowers was glued in, with an arrow pointing to the letters on the back. It explained the markings.

I guessed I should have gone back to reading it. But it was so much easier just to ask Tucker.

"Will Mom come for me again?"

"Your dad got a restraining order against her back then. I'm not sure whether it has expired. He may have called it off. You tried to have a relationship with her for a while."

"What's a restraining order?"

"It's something you can have the police use to keep people away from you. It's not as easy as it sounds. You have to prove they are a danger. Your dad had to hire a lawyer in your case to get it through. But it's one way of protecting yourself."

Protecting yourself. Flo at the diner had told me I should always do that. "What are the other ways?"

He sat back against the cushions. "You can learn self-defense. There are classes where you learn how to fight back, to hit and kick people, or to escape if someone grabs you."

I shifted forward, my mind a whirl, picturing myself kicking and hitting someone to get away. "Where can I do that?"

"I can look up a class for you and sign you up. There's bound to be some close enough to walk, or…" He trailed off.

My body tensed. Or what? I waited for him to keep going.

"I could drive you to a class. I don't mind."

"Okay."

He took a quick, short breath, as if he were surprised by my answer. "I'll find one. I guess I need to know your work schedule at the diner."

"Big Harry will let me work whenever I want." He'd said so.

"Okay. Good."

I flipped through more of the pages. "It's still hard to read. I get headaches."

"Yes, that happened before, too."

I kept turning pages. It was maddening, Tucker knowing more about me than I did. "Listening is easier."

"That's why we made the videos."

Was he right about everything?

"Okay, fine. Let's watch some videos. Then I guess we can start the date."

He grinned at that. "Let me go get the laptop."

CHAPTER 17
Tucker

I had to choose carefully. Ava had burned out on watching the videos during our hour visits, often slamming the laptop shut when she couldn't keep up.

As I returned to the living room with the laptop, I tried to remember the sequence we'd used in the previous resets. The first part would go a lot like it did with the video she gave Vinnie. Not that it had worked very well.

But Ava always started by establishing that she could read and understand using the tattoo. She'd explain who she was—a photographer. Where she lived—in Austin. And who the important people in her life were —me, her father, Big Harry, Maya.

In the last iteration of the sequence, we hadn't emphasized her mother, although we always mention Geneva due to the tattoo.

Then we included video clips showing where she lived, the people she'd talked about. We told stories together on camera. Laughed a lot, touched each other, to establish who she and I were. Kissed.

It was all there. It just took time and attention to get through it. Ava was always impatient with it.

When I sat down on the sofa, Ava was reading the messages she'd transcribed into the book.

"Learning anything good?" I asked her.

"I really didn't like my mother when I wrote these," she said. "Are there any videos with her in them? Or photos? I should know what she looks like if she tries to approach. It sounds like she came to Big Harry's once?"

I set the laptop on the table. "Yes. When you were looking for a job, she found where you'd posted in response to the diner's ad. We used Craig's List back then. She also showed up at your college when a fellow photography student posted an image with your real name."

"Real name? Do I have one that isn't real?"

"Yes, you go by Ava Flowers for your business and on your photo credits."

"Oh, that's interesting."

I opened the laptop. "You like to photograph flowers, plus you used to call Maya by Grandma Flowers when she lived next door to you and your mom. The name was an homage to her."

"Homage?"

"To honor her."

"I haven't met her yet."

"She's ready when you are. She knows you like to take it slow."

Ava peered at the laptop screen. "Do you have a video of my mother?"

I did. It's not what I would have preferred to show at this moment, but I clicked onto the folder for the sequence. "How much do you know about her so far?"

She flipped to the opening of her book. "I know I felt it was important to put her on the first page."

"It used to be more important than it is now. Your dad wasn't in the picture back then. You were on your own after you ran away."

"Give me a rundown of the worst of what she did."

I sat back against the cushions. "When we first met, you told me she would remove pages from your journals so you couldn't relearn anything she didn't want you to know. And sometimes she would substitute pages with her own words and pretend they were yours."

Ava pressed her hand to the tattoo. "Which is why I told myself to only trust this handwriting."

"Right. When you lose your memory, it is like a fresh start for everyone around you. They can decide what you should know about them."

"So, I started documenting everything I could so I would have a more complete picture."

"Exactly."

"What else did she do? You said she pretended I was fifteen when I was eighteen so I wouldn't leave home."

"There was that, for sure. But she also tried to get you declared medically incompetent in the children's hospital so you couldn't leave even at eighteen. That way, the police would bring you back if you ran away."

"Wow. I guess that failed."

"Yes. You were really smart in the hospital, and the social worker wouldn't sign off on it."

"When we met?"

"Yes, when we met."

"And you helped me."

I didn't want to overstate my role. "I tried."

She nodded. "Okay, is that it?"

"She got me arrested. She didn't want us to see each other. I taught you about the world, and she didn't want you to know anything, so you would have to rely on her. And she would move you whenever you made friends, hoping your memory would reset, and you would forget them."

"That's awful." Ava clasped her hands tightly together in her lap. "No wonder I got the tattoo."

"You tried to work with her after a reset when you were nineteen. Harry drove you out to her house because you wanted to move in with her. He didn't know not to."

She sits up tall. "Harry drove me there?"

"He didn't know. He does now. He would never do it again."

Ava stood up, pacing back and forth in front of the television. "Will she try to come for me? Was she invited to the wedding?"

I needed to bring her down. I could see her agitation rising. "She was not invited to the wedding. She got... pushy when you were twenty. She would show up at your apartment. She worries about you, maybe a little excessively."

"I see." Ava stopped walking. "But she's not a danger? Not a threat?"

"I don't think so. You might be vulnerable for a day or two after a memory reset, but once you have oriented yourself again, you know not to go anywhere with her."

"Would she kidnap me?"

I hesitated. Geneva had tried to take off with Ava the time Harry drove her home. "I don't think she'd push you into a white van and make off with you."

"But you don't know." Ava's hands tightened into fists

as she walked back and forth. "I need that self-defense class!"

"We'll get it done as soon as we can." I wanted to stand up, hold her close, comfort her, but I knew better than to try.

"But I don't know what she looks like!" She gestured to the window. "I might have just talked to her on the street!"

I reached over to wake up the laptop again. "Let's show you right now." I quickly scanned the files in the sequence folder and double-clicked one titled "Pruning roses with Ava's mom."

She sat next to me, closer this time.

The video started. I had filmed this one on my phone, sideways, before vertical videos became popular with TikTok and Reels.

Ava and Geneva kneeled in the dirt in front of the Wimberley house. Ava wore shorts and a T-shirt. Geneva had on one of her loose dresses. Their hair matched, long and brown and straight.

The front porch sagged beside them, and the paint on the exterior was peeling. But the rose bushes were vibrant in pink, white, and red.

"You have to deadhead them," Geneva said, popping a bloom off a branch. "That signals the plant to create a new bud."

Ava reached for a white one and tugged. White petals scattered on the ground. "Ouch!"

"Oh!" Geneva scooted closer and took Ava's hand. "Watch out for the thorns!"

Ava in the video looked at the camera, at me, in concern.

"It's not bleeding," Geneva said. "You'll be all right."

"You're okay," my voice said.

They returned to the plants.

Ava peered closely at the screen. "She looks like me."

"You always favored each other."

Ava pointed at Geneva's frown. "She doesn't seem very happy."

"I don't know everything about her life, but it seems she had a hard time growing up."

The video ended. "And then she made mine hard for me."

"It can be that way."

Ava closed the laptop. "That's enough."

I agreed. This had not set the stage for our first outing like I wanted. "I have some ideas for our date."

"Oh, right. That."

For a moment, I thought she'd try to get out of it, but she added, "You're dressed up. I should probably change." She gestured to her shorts and a T-shirt that read, "I shoot first and print the images later."

"Not necessarily. I wanted to cover my bases. Do you want to hear the list?"

"Sure." She kicked off her tennis shoes and sat cross-legged on the cushion.

"First, there are two traditional options. A movie or dinner. Or both. There is a new *Superman* film everyone says is good. Or since you like *Schitt's Creek*, you might like the *Naked Gun* remake."

"I haven't been to a movie theater yet. Joseph said *Superman* was good."

"For a movie, you can be dressed as you are. I wore this in case we went to a fancy restaurant."

"Did we used to do that? Eat fancy meals?"

I shook my head. "Only with your father. We have to budget for that sort of thing. Bills always came first."

"Oh, right." She jumped up. "There were some envelopes with your name on them."

I followed her to the kitchen. She had prepared a stack. "I know we have to pay all these things. I'm not sure how. I've been putting my money in here." She opened the junk drawer. It was stuffed with cash, probably from her tips.

"We pay for most things online, using a computer. We send a check in for a few of them, like rent."

"I assume we split these bills before? It doesn't seem fair if you aren't living here."

I don't want to tell her that there's no way she can afford this place on her own, just working at Harry's. It took both of us, and some good photography gigs for her, to get by.

"We'll figure it out." I can ask Marcus for help if I have to, not that I want to. Not at all. We'd be okay for a while.

She studied my face. "You look worried about this. So, maybe no fancy restaurant." She twisted her hair in her fingers, and for a moment, everything seemed normal. She and I were standing in our kitchen, trying to figure out how to pay a bill, and nothing else was the least bit hard. I held on to the moment for as long as possible, an oasis in the desert of the distance between us.

"Let's do the movie," she said. "But let me put on a different shirt or something. We look like Eve and Jared."

"Eve and Jared?"

"Oh, this couple who comes into the diner every day for lunch. Eve always wears these old jeans and a faded shirt. And Jared wears a suit."

The image made me smile. "That's fun. I'm guessing they are older?"

"I can't tell people's ages easily yet. But they aren't

gray or anything. They do seem older than me, though. Maybe like Harry?"

I got her meaning. "Okay, so choose something else to wear so we aren't Eve and Jared."

She took off to the bedroom.

I sorted through the envelopes, making a stack to take with me. We were stretched a little more than usual because of the wedding. Marcus had paid for the bulk of it, but we still had our own expenses. Her gifts to her sisters. Our rings. New suitcases for the trip.

I'd taken a week off from work. And Ava wasn't doing the job that had enabled us to move into a house.

It would be all right. I had to have faith.

When Ava came out in a yellow sundress, her brown hair brushing against her shoulders, my breath caught.

I did have faith. It was my job.

I would do anything for her. Literally anything.

Hopefully, this would be the first really good day since our failed wedding.

CHAPTER 18

Ava

My world had been pretty small since waking up in the limo. I'd been to the hospital, the blue house, the neighborhood, and taken the walk to Big Harry's Diner.

But that was it. That was all I knew.

Riding in the car with Tucker was a surprise a minute.

The road could go up into the air! It was like we were flying!

I clutched the door as we passed over the city. Entire buildings were below us, and other roads with cars crossed underneath.

"Isn't this terrifying?" I asked Tucker.

He laughed. "You get used to it."

I was relieved when we finally went down again with grass on either side of the street.

"There aren't any roads in the air on *Schitt's Creek*!" This couldn't be normal.

"That show is set in a very tiny town," he said. "Only cities have elevated roads."

We turned right, and a huge building loomed in front

of us, stretching on and on with parking lots the size of my entire neighborhood around it.

"What is this?"

"Barton Creek Mall," he said. "They're showing *Superman*. Plus, there are restaurants and stores inside. You can see a lot of things at once in a mall."

Mall. The word was familiar. I had a vague sense of the mall being a good place. A fun spot to go. But there were no malls in *Schitt's Creek* either. And I couldn't picture one.

"Nobody has talked about a mall at the diner."

"They are a dying breed," Tucker said. "Northcross Mall is gone. Highland Mall became part of the community college. We only have Barton Creek Mall and Lakeline Mall left."

"Why are they dying?"

"Online shopping has hurt them. There's a lot of empty indoor space that has to be maintained in a mall, which makes them expensive. Things like the Domain and the Hill Country Galleria, where the shops are all outside, are more popular."

I peeled my sweating thigh off the vinyl seat. It was seriously hot outside today, and Tucker's car hadn't cooled down much despite the air blowing on us. "Why would anyone want to be outside when they could be inside?"

"That's a question I often ask myself. I love malls."

Tucker parked the car, and we walked the long stretch to the big glass doors. People streamed into the building, which had two levels.

We entered next to a long desk with movie posters on screens above it. I spotted *Superman*, as well as the *Naked Gun* movie Tucker had mentioned.

"Thirteen dollars to see a movie?" I asked him. "I only

get four dollars in tips at a typical table. So, I have to serve four of them just to watch a movie?"

Tucker walked up to a screen and tapped the glass. "Life is expensive."

"Maybe we should walk around. That doesn't cost anything, does it?"

He paused. "We can do that. But we can afford a movie."

"Do you make more money than four dollars a table?"

"We have a budget that shows how much we earn and how much everything costs. We could look at it when we go home."

"Okay."

"Should I buy tickets?" he asked.

I stuffed down my concern. Tucker surely knew what we could do. "Yes. Okay."

But when we went inside and I saw the prices of drinks and popcorn, I said, "No way. I bought popcorn at the store. It was five dollars for six bags. They are charging ten dollars for one!"

Tucker laughed. "Pretty much everyone agrees with you there."

We walked along a long hall to the door with the number that the man checking our tickets said was ours.

Inside, the air was frigid. After the hot car ride, it was pure bliss.

We walked up a ramp, then I stopped so suddenly that Tucker almost ran into me.

"You okay?" he asked.

But I couldn't believe what I was seeing. It was a TV screen, but it filled an entire wall. I turned to him. "How did they make it so big?"

"It's actually a big surface where they project the image. There were movies like this before there were televisions."

"Really? They shrunk the screens? Why don't we have something this big at home?"

He passed me. "Some people do."

"I want to do that." I followed him up a few stairs to a row of big, cushioned chairs.

When I sat on one next to him, it was like settling onto my sofa. "This is great!"

"It gets better." He pushed a button next to my arm, and the back moved down, and my feet moved up!

I gasped. "You could sleep on this!"

"You might if the movie gets boring."

I pushed the button again and again, moving up and down, until someone sat in the chair next to me and frowned.

I giggled and moved closer to Tucker, not that I could reach him. The chairs had wide arms. "I think I annoyed her," I whispered.

"It's all right," he said.

The screen was flashing images of various businesses, but then suddenly, music came on, so loud I had to cover my ears.

A woman filled the screen. "I'm Maria Menounos," she said. "And this is Noovie, your pre-movie entertainment."

Tucker leaned over. "You'll get used to the sound. It's startling at first."

"Why is it so loud?"

"Some people are hard of hearing."

I tried to parse that phrase. Hard to hear, maybe he meant? But he was right. As Maria kept talking, asking us trivia questions about movies I'd never heard of, I was able to uncover my ears.

Everyone around us had drinks and popcorn, rattling wrappers. The smell was heavenly.

Tucker noticed me staring. "What if we shared? Then it would be like half-price. You love popcorn."

I did. I was drawn to the boxes in my cabinet. Harry showed me how to microwave them. When we ran out, I replaced them the first time Harry took me to the store.

"Okay," I said.

"Do you want to wait here? I'll be right back."

I glanced around. "Yes. I will be all right."

He crossed in front of me. I watched the huge screen flash colors and light. Maria was beautiful, and I kept wanting to shift my shoulders like she did to angle my head and chin. The only person I'd seen as beautiful as her was Alexis on *Schitt's Creek*.

Tucker returned. "Here you go." He handed me a bucket of popcorn and set a drink in a holder between us.

"Oh, that's a lot of popcorn!" The smell of the butter and salt made me want to shove my face into the kernels.

"Wait until you try it. There's no popcorn like movie popcorn."

I picked up a few pieces and popped them into my mouth.

Oh. Oh! Tucker was right. The flavor was so much more intense. More salt. More butter. I wanted to scoop up huge handfuls.

"Good, right?" he said.

"We should have done this before!" I said.

He smiled. "We can do it whenever we like."

"You mean whenever we can pay for it."

"That, too."

I angled the bucket toward him to share. Maria said goodbye until next time, and my whole body rumbled as the noise levels lifted with a scene of a lone woman in a beautiful pink dress with pale blonde hair.

I sat up, unable to look away. I had never felt like this before, like everything inside me was bursting to get out.

And then she started singing. And a woman with a green face and a pointy hat flew down on a broom.

They sang to each other, and I forgot about the popcorn, the seat that moved, and Tucker beside me. I started crying. Everything was so beautiful and sad and wonderful and sharp.

I couldn't contain everything I felt. My chest was so full. When finally, the screen went black with the words, "Coming in November," I turned to Tucker. "What just happened?"

"It's a powerful movie. We'll watch the first one and then come back in November for the second."

I reached out to squeeze my hand, and I clutched it like the one thing that I knew was familiar.

Other scenes came on, and some of them were bright or intense. One made everyone laugh, but I couldn't follow it. Everything happened too fast.

But then there was another pause, and a strange stillness came over the theater, like everyone was finally paying attention.

Tucker leaned over. "*Superman* is starting."

I pushed the button to lift my feet a little more. I was full of popcorn, and there was so much left. I balanced it on my belly. It didn't matter anymore if *Superman* was a good movie or not. I had already experienced what it was like to live another life and feel things like other people, just from the short pieces I'd watched.

I grabbed hold of Tucker's hand in case the feelings got that strong again.

I loved this entire experience so far, even the parts I didn't quite understand. No matter what else we did today, this was really, really good.

CHAPTER 19

Tucker

I was holding Ava's hand.

It had been weeks since I had gotten to touch her in any meaningful way. She was overwhelmed by the trailer for *Wicked*. It was a powerful soundtrack and a beautiful scene. I was glad she'd gotten to experience it.

Seeing it, feeling it, would awaken the artist in her. Vinnie had told me she was struggling with the photos. She didn't know what to take pictures of. She didn't see the point. I had been surprised to see her walk up with her camera when I arrived for the date.

But I was willing to bet that after today she would start to see the beauty in everything again. Survivor Ava would shift to the back of her mind, and she would move forward with her own unique vision of what the world, *her world*, should look like.

I couldn't wait. It was the best part of being with Ava.

I paid more attention to her than to the movie. She squeezed my fingers when the story got tense, when Superman was trapped by the enemy, and there seemed no way out.

She laughed at the dog. She cried when Superman sat with his father, feeling defeated.

She had no filters, no protections, not yet. She would feel everything deeply, both good and bad. That was why toddlers cried when they were startled. They couldn't suppress the intensity of their reaction. It felt like near death to them.

She was the same, although she had more control of her body and could adjust more quickly than a two-year-old.

Eventually, she let go of me to take a drink of the soda. By the time we got to the end, she had steadied her emotions again. "That was good. Are all movies like this?"

I picked up the cup and the mostly empty bucket. "No. Some movies are not good at all. But this one was."

We exited the theater with the others, blinking when we got out into the light.

"To the mall?" she said. "I saw all the stores when you were buying the tickets."

"Absolutely." I would extend this date for as long as possible.

She took my hand again as we approached the mob of people outside the theater. I wanted to hold on to this moment. Ava and I, wandering the mall like any other couple. No failed wedding. No starting over. No having to leave my house.

We were getting another new beginning.

It was our sixth.

We got home hours later, feet sore from walking the mall, stuffed with Annie's pretzels, Dippin' Dots, and boba tea.

We'd bought goofy sunglasses at Spencer's, a Totoro umbrella at Hot Topic, and a perfume at Dillard's that Ava had dragged me back three times to sniff again.

We were teenagers, impulsive, silly. We laughed a lot.

It was only when we got to the yellow door of our blue house that I remembered I wasn't allowed inside without an invitation. I couldn't take her hand and lead her to the sofa to watch TV or to our bedroom.

I couldn't even kiss her. Not without risking the momentum I'd gained.

When she unlocked the door, she said, "I'll run in and get the envelopes for you."

Well, that was that. I waited on the porch, trying to hang on to the joy of the day. But the disappointment of having to leave her encroached.

She popped back out with the stack. "It was a good day. Can we go to another movie soon?"

"Of course. I'll text you with some ideas, or you can look."

She nodded. Her face was beaming. She felt no angst about this moment by the door. She had no context for what I might expect, no worry if we should kiss or not, or what that could lead to.

"Well, okay, goodnight!" She passed me the envelopes.

And with that, she bounced back inside and closed the door.

I stood there for a moment, listening to the cicadas sing from the bushes. The night was warm and still. Down the street, someone started a car. A dog barked from a yard.

She hadn't locked the door. I resisted the urge to lock it myself with my key, but instead, I went down the steps to the sidewalk.

Even so, I sat in my car for long minutes, looking up at

her house, our house. How long would it take to get her back? The risk was always that she might meet some other man in these vulnerable first weeks and months. What would I do if she fell in love with someone else?

I had to believe. I pressed my palm to my collarbone, where the infinity tattoo inked my skin. We had gotten them in the good times to prepare for exactly these moments.

I could not consider any future that didn't include her, where we weren't together.

I would get her back. Tonight had been a solid first step.

When I got to Gram's, she was sitting with a cup of tea at the table in the kitchen.

"How did it go with Ava?"

"We saw *Superman* and walked around the mall. It was fun, like a high school date."

"Good, good. It's always slow going, isn't it?"

I sat down opposite her. "Seems to be."

"You are exactly the right person to do this for her, Tucker." Gram reached across the table to take my hand. "You always had all the determination in the world. She needs that."

I knew Gram was right. From the first moment I'd seen her in the disco room at the children's hospital, we'd been drawn to each other.

She'd trusted me from the beginning, in the swirling lights, and even the next day when she met me all over again.

Why was it harder now? She couldn't be different.

It was me. My expectations. My foreknowledge.

Even when my brain knew she didn't recognize me,

remember me, or know how she once felt, my heart insisted she should.

Hell, we'd tattooed it on our skin.

The heart remembers.

So, why was it so difficult? Why did it take so long?

And why was it so hard to bear?

CHAPTER 20

Ava

Dating was fun.

Tucker took me to a food truck park where we could choose from tacos or sushi or gyros or burgers. I picked cupcakes. Tucker agreed that life was uncertain, so dessert first all around.

We saw more movies. And went bowling, which I figured out I'd done before when I rolled the ball and knocked all but two pins down on the first try.

"Muscle memory," Tucker said. "You were always a good bowler."

I wondered what other skills I had.

He lingered more and more at the door when these dates were over. One day at Harry's, I finally asked Flo about it.

"What would make Tucker stand by the front door for like forever when we go home?"

She laughed, using her phone camera to apply a layer of bright red lip gloss. Flo was thirty-six and cared a lot about her makeup being "on point" and that her bleached blonde curls never frizzed. "Girl, he's on the prowl, of course, he is. He hasn't gotten any since your wedding day, and he's bound to be getting blue in the balls."

Harry passed by for the last part and stopped dead in his tracks. "Flo, mind yer business and clear those tables."

Flo popped her hip in tight white jeans. "Aww, why can't Jimmie do it? What's the point of a busboy if we have to bus ourselves?"

"Everybody buses," Harry said, his voice dark and low.

"Oh, listen to you, you big ol' bear." Flo flounced off but not toward the tables. She was probably off to find Jimmie to do it.

Harry sighed. "Don't listen to Flo. She's never had a man like Tucker and definitely not a situation like yours."

I stacked plates, mindful of the forks so they wouldn't fly off the edge. I wanted to ask him what Tucker hadn't gotten any of and what balls would be blue? Like the gumballs in the little machines by the door? Some of those were blue.

I told him, "I didn't understand a word she said."

"Probably for the best," Harry said and moved to the bar, where a customer was waiting.

So, he was no help.

But maybe I got the idea. People in the movies were always kissing or getting into bed together. I wasn't sure exactly how it worked. I could probably Google it.

I know Tucker and I slept together in the bed in our house. And I did feel things when I was with him.

I was just…scared. Those emotions were hard to contain. Superman and Lois had an epic fight about relationships. And David Rose and Stevie and Patrick were always mixing it up on the show. Not to mention Alexis and Mutt and then Ted.

These things were complicated. And I had no one to ask. Harry didn't feel right. Flo was full of advice I didn't understand. I didn't talk to the other servers long enough for something so serious.

Maybe I could ask Vinnie. Or bring it up to Tucker. That made the most sense.

I carried the plates to the back. I was getting off work, anyway. As I put my apron in my cubby and gathered my purse and keys, Flo walked up. She pulled a magazine from her slot. Flo loved magazines, thick and glossy with inserts that fell out. She called herself "old school" and said that "no over-hyped influencer" would ever replace the "good ol' mags."

"You need this more than me," she said, handing me a thick copy of *Cosmopolitan*. She pointed to the type on the front and read it aloud. "How to figure out the average man."

Oh! That did sound helpful. "I'll bring it back," I told her.

"No matter. I've read that one cover to cover. The new one comes out tomorrow."

I tucked it under my arm. "Thanks."

"We girls gotta watch out for each other. If that boyfriend of yours wants to stick it in you, you make sure he knows what's in it for you."

"I'll, uh, do that. Thanks."

I waited until I had crossed First Street, which was wild with cars late afternoon, to open the magazine and look.

The women were so perfect, and their clothes fit so well. The men were attentive, often tripping over themselves in the presence of the ladies. Tucker was like that, just not wearing those outfits.

Something tickled the back of my neck as I meandered

down the sidewalk, dodging other walkers and people riding scooters.

I glanced around. This part of the street was always busy. Buses. Long lines of traffic sat impatiently at each light. The exhaust was strong. Maybe I'd turn off early. It was a solid mile walk to my house from here.

I had my magazine to keep me company.

I relaxed as I left the busy street behind.

But then my neck tickled again.

What was causing that?

I stopped abruptly and turned around.

A woman in a long flowy dress walked half a block behind me. I recognized her from the rose video. "Mother?"

She froze, glancing around. "You know who I am?"

"Of course, I do. Geneva Roberts. You ruined my childhood."

She pressed her hand against her chest. She looked older than in the video I'd seen, her shoulder-length brown hair sparkling gray in the afternoon light. There were lines around her eyes.

I tried to breathe through my alarm. My tattoo flitted through my vision. *Mom is bad.*

"Why are you following me?" I asked.

"I was—hoping to catch you. I thought you might be working at Big Harry's again."

We stood well apart, enough that we had to raise our voices to hear each other. No one walked this part of the neighborhood. The row of houses was silent and still.

"What do you want?" I asked her.

She took a step toward me, but I took a step back. She stopped. "I would never hurt you. You are my only child. The most important thing to me."

"Right. That's why you never wanted me to leave."

She attempted to flash a smile, but I wasn't fooled.

"Ava, I wanted to ask how your wedding went."

"You weren't invited."

"I know. But I knew of it. Your father posted your engagement in the Houston paper." She dug through a tattered bag on her elbow and pulled out a clipping. "He seems very proud."

I had seen the newspaper announcement. Father had showed it to me on one of his visits since the wedding. The image he used of Tucker and me was one I had taken. A color copy of it hung on the wall of the bedroom.

I almost told her the wedding hadn't happened, but that weird tingle came back, so I stayed silent.

"It didn't happen, did it?" she asked in a tone that told me she already knew the answer. This was all a ruse.

I turned around and began walking. I should have taken self-defense classes right away. Tucker was supposed to find one.

I'd find a class on my own.

I hurried for two more blocks before I sensed she was still behind me. I was leading her right to my house. I halted and turned around.

Her face was red, and sweat made her hair damp around the edges. Walking fast was hard for her. "I won't hurt you, Ava."

"I read all about you."

"You seem different. Have you lost your memory recently?"

I didn't want to answer that either, but I felt stuck. I couldn't walk home. She'd know where I live. Maybe I should go back to Harry's.

She pressed a tissue to her forehead. "I'm guessing you

have. And that's why the wedding didn't take place." She gripped the purse handle with both hands. "I checked the public records. Your marriage certificate was never filed."

So, she'd checked up on me.

"Please go away."

"Ava, you're a grown woman. I have no power over you."

Not true. "If you hid me away somewhere, stopped me from taking my meds, I would eventually have a seizure and forget where I was supposed to be. You could tell me anything. You were good at that."

"You always were so very smart," she said. "I just—I had hoped—"

"Whatever it is you want, I can't give it to you," I said. "If I feel safe later, maybe we can have lunch or something. But right now, I'm trying to rebuild my life."

"I'm so sorry it happened again," she said. "If you would listen to me, the treatments I found were better."

"Right, because I had so many fewer seizures with you." I left the sidewalk and went into the street. I would cross it here and head back toward Harry's. This wasn't safe at all.

"When you were growing up, sure." Her voice took on a pleading tone. "Ava, please listen. You went a long time with no trouble until you ran away. There are studies on what I was doing. It's a real treatment!"

I didn't know what she was talking about, and I wouldn't believe anything she said without asking my father first.

I walked swiftly toward First Street.

"Ava, you have my number on your phone. If you keep struggling, please consider what I have to say."

I waved her off, hurrying toward the busier street, to people I knew.

She stood in place for as long as I walked. Eventually, I turned a corner, and I couldn't see her anymore.

When I was far enough away, my belly shook so hard that my teeth chattered. When I got to Harry's, I didn't go in, but I sat on a bench, watching for her to emerge from the neighborhood.

She never did.

Eventually, I went in a different direction to home, constantly watching over my shoulder.

I pressed my hand against my hip, over the tattoo, hidden beneath my jeans. I wouldn't have put it there if I hadn't meant it.

CHAPTER 21

Tucker

Ava got spooked enough by an encounter with her mother that I immediately signed her up for self-defense.

I offered to take it with her, but she said I might be someone she needed to defend herself from, and if I learned it, she would never win.

While I was quite sure Ava could kick my butt, class or not, I understood her fear. I wouldn't do anything that made things worse for her. So, I drove her to class and sat in the car to wait for her to be done.

During those hours, I took the time to read more about other amnesiacs' recoveries. I already knew that the visual, auditory, and other sensory memories were all stored differently. What I wanted to know was the techniques that would help her reconnect her present circumstances to her old emotions.

Smells were the strongest, the research showed. A perfume, a favorite food, or the unique combination of scents of a specific place could evoke the feeling of a memory, even if the actual event could not be accessed.

It was important, though, that the smell be unique. If a cleaning fluid or a brand of cat litter or the whiff of the same lavender candle became commonplace, there was no way to access an emotion or even a sense of familiarity.

But I had ideas. If her brain couldn't remember the life we'd built together, maybe her nose and stomach would.

The dates had gone well. But popcorn had gotten overused. And we'd been to most of the old places. Despite so much more time together, we were staying friendly. I couldn't make any inroads into her heart. I might as well be Big Harry. Or Vinnie.

But I would work on it. On our next night together, I brought over a bag of groceries.

She let me into the house, her curiosity already urging her to peek at what was inside. "What's all that?"

"I'm going to make us dinner," I said.

"Good idea," she said. "It costs less money, plus, we get leftovers."

Survival Ava. We'd gone over our budget the week before, and she was aghast at how close we were cutting it. She redoubled her efforts to get her photography back to her old standard so she could earn more than she did at Harry's.

"What are we having?" she asked.

"Lasagna." This was once her favorite dish. It had served us well, getting us back together when she was nineteen. It had become shorthand for us over the years for when either of us wanted to get busy. *Are we having lasagna tonight? Should we make lasagna? It's been a while since we had lasagna.*

"Have you made it for me before?" she asked. "We don't serve that at Harry's."

This, I knew. And we hadn't been to an Italian restaurant on a date. This would be new to her. "Not for a long time." The lasagna I made from Gram's recipe would evoke many good feelings, a true connection that ran deeper than friendship. It was the only ace in my hand.

She followed me to the kitchen. "I know the word lasagna, but I can't picture it. Can you describe it to me?"

I began pulling the boxes and jars as I explained.

"It's done in layers. First, you boil these long, flat noodles." I held up the blue box. "And then you make the sauce." I showed her the bag of tomatoes and began pulling spices from the rack on the wall.

"You're using a lot of those," she said. "I haven't touched them."

She'd been mainly reheating frozen meals or leftovers from Harry's. "You'll like how it all works together." I pulled out packages of ricotta, mozzarella, and freshly grated Parmesan.

She examined the spread. "That's a lot of cheese."

"That's what makes it so good. You layer the pasta, cheese, and meat sauce. Then you bake it. Would you like to make it with me, so you learn how?"

She glanced around the kitchen. So much of it was still foreign to her. She could pick up pots and pans and spoons and knives and know what they were, but the alchemy of cooking, remembering recipes, and portioning out the right amounts of ingredients were skills still well beyond her.

"All right," she said. "I guess this is as good a day as any to learn how to feed myself properly."

I pulled out the cutting board and a chef's knife.

"That's a big knife," Ava said. "Want to see what I've learned?"

I turned to her, holding the knife.

She squatted, eyes on the blade, then suddenly her tennis shoe was flying at me, knocking the knife from my hand. It clattered to the floor.

She leaped into the hair and smacked her hands together. "I did it!"

"Nice moves," I told her, bending to pick it up.

"I'll wash it. I knocked it down." She reached for the handle, and our hands collided.

The jolt of touching her rocked through me like it had since the first date. She seemed to have gotten used to the regularity of our holding hands, but this time, her eyes went wide.

"*Cosmopolitan* talked about this," she said.

"The magazine?"

"Never mind." She took the knife and moved to the sink.

Interesting. *Cosmopolitan* would certainly have given her a lot of ideas she may not have had before.

I piled the tomatoes next to the sink, and she washed those, too.

She lifted one to inspect it. "Working at Harry's has taught me a few things. Mainly to make sure everything is clean."

I moved the tomatoes to the cutting board and took the knife, cutting an X into the ends. Then I peeled the paper off a head of garlic and pulled out several cloves. I used the flat edge of the knife to crush it.

Ava leaned on the counter. "You're good at that."

"I've had a lot of practice. Gram said she'd rather roll over dead than use bottled sauce."

"We have huge cans of it at Harry's."

"It's a common shortcut." I bent down to retrieve the

big stew pot and dump the tomatoes in. I covered them with water and started the flame.

Ava opened the end of the pasta box, admiring the long, flat pieces. "Did we used to make lasagna together?"

"I would make it for you."

"And I liked it?"

"It was one of our favorite meals."

While the tomatoes boiled enough to be skinned, I found the bottle of olive oil in the cabinet next to the stove and swirled a couple of tablespoons along the bottom of a pan. When I dropped the garlic into the hot oil, the entire kitchen filled with the fragrant aroma.

"Ooooh," Ava said. "That smells so good." She scooted closer.

I sprinkled in all the other spices, each one adding to the unique smell of the sauce. I watched her as I went along.

"This is making me so hungry," she said. "And happy!"

"Can you put some ice and water in a bowl?"

"Sure!" She pulled out a big mixing bowl and filled it. "What's this for?"

I used a spoon to pull the tomatoes out of the boiling water and into the ice bath. "This will make them shrink so I can pull the skins off."

"This sure is a lot of work."

"It's worth it."

We peeled the tomatoes together, laughing at how slippery they were. The next time our hands collided in the bowl, her gaze snapped to mine. She wasn't laughing now. Something had caught within her, and she was surprised at the feeling.

It was working. This was exactly how we used to be.

While the sauce cooked, I told her we should listen to some music.

"Yes!" Ava cried. "I found the music on my phone. Flo said my collection was 'eclectic.' I think she meant it as an insult."

"We are all over the place."

She pressed play, dancing around the room to Lizzo from the speaker on the phone. But we had a better setup than that. I moved to a shelf near the back door, where a Bluetooth speaker was plugged into the wall. When I powered it on, it automatically hooked into her phone, and the song poured from it, pure and loud.

"Yes!" Ava cried, waving her arms and turning in circles.

The music stayed upbeat for a few songs, then toned down. The smell of the sauce filled the space. We spun around the table for the fast songs, and finally, when a somber Taylor Swift ballad came on, Ava laid her arms on my shoulders. We moved together slowly through the kitchen.

She let everything come over her. The smells, the words, the ribbon of music winding its way through her senses.

"I like you, Tucker Giddings," she said. "*Cosmo* said you were supposed to kiss me by the third date. This is like seven or eight."

I did not waste any time. I drew her close against me, both my hands holding her head. I bent down and pressed my mouth to hers.

Sixth first kiss.

This part was the same. The fit of our lips. The tilt of her face. Her fingers gripped my shoulders. It was as though no time had passed since the last time I'd kissed her, since the morning of our wedding day.

She wasn't tentative at all. There was no war in her head about things being too fast or too slow. She was completely in the moment, letting her body be her guide.

She pressed against me, chest to chest, hips to hips. I knew when she felt something different about me because she pulled back, her eyebrows lifted. "I read about that part. I have to make sure you know what's in it for me."

I laughed. So, maybe she did have a few things swirling in her head. "Ava, trust me, everything we do is all about you."

"I'm supposed to play hard to get, at least a little." She pushed on my chest to separate us. "What happens next with lasagna?"

I led her back to the stove to start the water for the noodles.

But this time, we worked on it together, arm in arm, kissing in between.

The terrible tension in my chest started to ease.

I was getting her back.

For the next few nights, we planned dishes and cooked them together. I loved this because it was a facet of our relationship that hadn't existed before. We always took turns with the dinners, letting the other person work or relax.

Now, teamwork in the kitchen was our new normal.

Fresh vegetables and salads and ingredients turned a simple meal into memories for her. We had more than just the food. We had research, conversations, and planning.

This simple act of setting out and achieving a goal with a new recipe boosted her confidence. She relaxed more and worried less. We curled up on the sofa to eat and watch a movie, often old classics that weren't too flashy or loud.

About two weeks into our new culinary relationship, I suggested we take a night off and let someone else cook for us. We hadn't been to a nice restaurant since she'd lost her memory because she obsessed over every expenditure now that she had seen the budget.

But one of my buddies at the garage told me about this hole-in-the-wall Italian place that wasn't too expensive, had good food, and had a very romantic vibe. He assured me it was quiet and small.

When we went out to the car to go, she asked to drive, another surprise. Her doctor told her it was okay if another adult was in the car.

She did a good job navigating the side streets and remembering when to signal and when to change lanes. I worked hard to make it fun and easy for her, suppressing any feelings I had of alarm if she braked too hard or passed a turn.

Her sense of accomplishment was written all over her face. "I'm back on the road! Six weeks until I can drive on my own!"

When we walked inside the restaurant, she loved the place immediately. "It's like in *Casablanca*! We're in the movie."

I had to agree with her here. In the corner, a man played an upright piano. The music heightened the charming, old-fashioned feel of the place with its nestled tables and antique decor.

We sat near the music, and she asked the man at the piano to play "As Time Goes By." He gave her a half-smile.

No doubt he was asked to play that song many times every night. I dropped some cash in this tip jar, and we settled at our table, close together, tucked against a wall draped with red velvet.

We talked about the menu, and she settled on their lasagna so we could compare it to our own. I chose some things I thought she might like to try, and we talked easily about the photos she'd been taking with Vinnie, my job, and the meals we would likely make next week.

Our lives were very small. Without the breadth and depth of her history, we could only speak of things that had happened in the last month. Just like the previous time she'd lost her memory, Ava had little interest in her forgotten past. She wanted to move forward, only focusing on the elements of her knowledge that she needed to help her with her present.

I ordered Baked Alaska for our dessert, and she clapped like a girl when the server lit the top on fire.

"I can't believe it!" she said. "I've never had a dessert that caught on fire before!"

We had, more than once, but there was no need to tell her that. I smiled at her delight and dipped my spoon inside the ice cream to feed her a bite out of habit.

Her excitement about the new experience was high enough that she did not question me feeding her but leaned forward to accept it. I watched her swallow the bite, her eyes on me. Her comfort with me was growing.

"It's really good," she said. "It makes me feel funny inside."

I knew the dessert wasn't what was making her feel strange, but I simply nodded. I took a bite myself from the same spoon. She noticed, and her eyebrows lifted. But when I offered another bite to her on the same spoon again, she still took it.

This simple intimacy opened the door to get her closer to me. I pulled some notes from my adolescent playbook, turning on a scary movie after dinner so she would clutch my arm. I smiled when she grabbed hold of me but did not let go even when the frightening part had passed.

This was real progress.

CHAPTER 22

Ava

Tucker was good. Life with him was easy again.

My photography, however, was slow going.

One Friday, Vinnie and I sat at the don't-drink-coffee table and reviewed prints of photos I'd taken of people at a park. Most of them were of him in various light situations. Full sun, partial shade, full shade. But we'd run into a family who came to Big Harry's fairly often, and they were willing to let me practice on them.

"So, look at my nose in this one versus this one," Vinnie said, putting two images of him side by side. "Can you see the difference?"

"Your nose is huge in that one," I said. "Like it got squashed."

"My nose is a thing of beauty," Vinnie said with a laugh. "But if you flash it directly from the front, it will destroy my Calvin Klein aesthetic."

Fortunately, I'd seen Calvin Klein ads in Flo's magazine, so I knew what he was trying to say. I sometimes studied the photographs in those, looking at the poses, the shadows, the light sources. I took confusing ones to Vinnie to decipher, and he said, "Oh, that is just some bad Photoshop work."

Photoshop was an entirely different beast. I was expected to get rid of blemishes and bruises. Vinnie had showed me how to use a digital pen to push in a roll of skin that spilled out over a waistband or to minimize a double chin.

That seemed like cheating to me, but Vinnie said people didn't pay big bucks for professional photographers to look like their iPhone photos. They wanted to see the very best versions of themselves.

I preferred the flowers and the animals to people, but Vinnie said editorial work or photographic art was not an easy way to pay the bills.

And bills were important. Old Ava had worried a lot about covering rent and electric and making it on her own. It was all over her scrapbook. I was starting to understand it.

"Do you and Tucker have a date tonight?" Vinnie asked, gathering the photos.

"Yes, we're making chicken spaghetti, which I had to ask about because I didn't see how to make long skinny noodles out of chicken meat."

Vinnie laughed. "Ava, Mija, you are a card."

I'd come to understand that cards and decks of cards and card games were a popular way to describe situations. Maybe I would have Tucker teach me how to play.

"Vinnie, have I always used Ava Flowers for my pictures instead of my real name?" He'd known me since community college at ACC.

"No. I met you as Ava Roberts, and when you are in a class, you don't get to use a fake name. But then that tonto in Fundamentals of Studio Lighting uploaded an image of you and tagged your name in it." Vinnie used his hands to make great flourishes in the air. "Your mother showed up from nowhere like la bruja, and you got very spooked."

Only Tucker knew about the incident with my mother following me. "I saw her a few weeks ago."

Vinnie hands froze in midair. "Where?"

"Walking home. She was in the neighborhood."

Vinnie touched his forehead and both shoulders. "What did she say?"

"She tried to convince me to do some other treatment. She knew the wedding hadn't happened."

Vinnie shook his head. "She's checking up on you. Be careful, Mija."

"I know. I'm taking self-defense classes."

He nodded. "Good. She's a real *Mommie Dearest*. Be very careful."

"*Mommie Dearest*?"

"It's a movie about a very bad mother. One of the classics." Vinnie slid the images into an envelope. "I think you're ready to do a real shoot. You want to try?"

"When?"

"Saturday evening. The golden hour. Seven, as the sun goes now. Zilker Park."

I'd read about that park. Tucker and I went there on our second date. "Okay. Sure."

"I will come for you at six-fifteen. Wear jeans. We kneel a lot. There are niños involved."

Now, I got it. "You don't love kids."

Vinnie stood up and lifted his camera bag. "They are good money, of course. They order so much. But you definitely handle them better. And you did so good on these!" He tapped the envelope. "With the littles, it's more about personality than anything. They are tyrants and drive me loco."

"I bet so." Huh. That phrase had popped out of me. A bet. Back to cards again.

He headed for the door. "See you Saturday!"

When he left, I pulled out the photos to look over the images I'd taken of the children. They laughed, clutching their bellies, or did silly poses. It was very different from the more formal posing Vinnie himself had done. I guessed I was ready. I liked the kids better than the adults, anyway.

I flopped back onto the sofa. Tucker wasn't due for over an hour for dinner. I could watch something. I'd run out of *Schitt's Creek*.

On a whim, I pulled up the search function and typed in *Mommie Dearest*. Might be interesting to compare someone else's bad mom to mine.

Within an hour, I knew I shouldn't have watched it. She locked Christina in a room. She cut off her hair. She controlled her by being nice and then by being mean. She took her daughter's dolls, like mine had taken my journals.

Tucker came over while it was on, and I didn't even go to the door, curled up in a ball on the corner of the sofa.

When he sat down, the mother was hitting the little girl with coat hangers. I couldn't move, my nose buried in my knees, but my eyes glued to the screen.

Tucker snatched the remote and tried to turn it off, but I'd shouted at him not to. There were some things I needed to see.

He held onto me as we finished it out. I was relieved when the mother died.

"You mother wasn't like that," he said as the screen

went dark. "She didn't hit you. But she undermined you like that one. She made you feel uncertain and unsafe."

"Do you think the movie mother is worse than mine?" I relaxed into his embrace.

"I think they're both pretty awful." He squeezed my shoulders. "Did you ever tell your dad you saw your mom?"

"No. I didn't want him to make me move to Houston."

He drew me close to him again. "I'm glad. You can handle anything. You kicked a knife out of my hand, remember?"

"I do."

He stroked my hair. "You go through more than anybody I know."

I curled against his shoulder. "But you. Your mother and father. Your brother."

"But that's over. I got through it. You live with your challenges every day."

He was right. "Tell me about your mother. I want to hear about a good one."

His body tensed next to mine, and I almost wished I hadn't asked. But then it relaxed again. "She was a great mom. She was strict, you know. We had to clean up after ourselves. And she was forever telling us not to leave toothpaste in the sink."

"I do that sometimes," I said.

"You always have." He touched the tip of my nose. "It's cute."

Something else about old Ava I had retained. "What else?"

"She loved baking things. Cookies. Pies. Cakes. Dad always said she was going to fatten us all up."

"Did she?"

"Nah. We were busy. Yard work. Dad and Stephen had sports. She did Jazzercise."

"We haven't baked anything like that. Just dinners."

"We could. I could get things for a pie."

"Did I have a favorite before?"

"Cherry. Always cherry."

We had cherry pie at Big Harry's, but I'd never tried it. "I didn't know that."

"Once you eat it, you'll remember."

"Well, not exactly *remember*." I socked his arm.

"Your mouth will remember."

"Is that better than my heart?"

His face got all serious at that. "The heart is protective. Maybe the mouth has an easier time."

Did it? I had spit out a thing or two that I hadn't wanted to eat. I was in the *cilantro is soap* camp. And tapioca pudding made me gag. Maybe my heart did the same thing, at least at first, when it was being protective. Spit things out. Made me want to get away.

But I was better. I wasn't scared all the time.

Other than when Mother showed up unexpectedly.

That had been bad. I wondered what she would do if I called her that.

Mommie Dearest.

CHAPTER 23

Tucker

One of the guys at the garage clued me into a movie I had never heard about. He said it was called *50 First Dates* and starred Adam Sandler and Drew Barrymore. The girl in the movie loses her memory every time she wakes up in the morning, and the guy has to convince her to fall in love with him all over again.

I watched the movie by myself at Gram's before I introduced it to Ava. When I was sure that it was a good idea, I planned a whole evening around it. We made some Hawaiian dishes and blended fruity drinks, the virgin version, because alcohol didn't play nice with Ava's medication.

She giggled at the little umbrellas that I tucked in each glass. We sat down to watch the movie together.

I'm sure she didn't laugh as much as the average person. She kept leaning forward and watching Drew Barrymore's face. Every once in a while, she made a comment like, "That guy sure is determined to make her like him as much as she did the first time."

And later, "That's funny about how they have their

first kiss over and over again."

I caught some side-eye with that one, as if she was just now realizing how many first kisses she and I had already had.

As the credits rolled, we sat in the half-dark of the screen, curled up together.

Eventually, she said, "Do I kiss the same as I did the other times?"

That was quite a question. "I'm usually too stressed out about it to notice."

She turned to me. "Really? Why?"

"Well, the first time, we were in front of your mother and hospital staff. You grabbed my face and snogged me."

"Snogged?"

"It's a British word for kissing."

"I don't like it. It sounds like a combination of snot and fog, and both are not good to think about when kissing."

I laughed. "You're right."

"What about the second one?"

"That one was on a Ferris wheel at a carnival."

"Oh, I saw the tickets in the scrapbook. Was it hard to get me to kiss you that time?"

"Terribly. You wanted nothing to do with me after you ran away from your mother's house."

"Yeah, that part of the scrapbook is hard to read."

"That's why I added sticky notes. It's important to understand that her part of your life is over."

"I didn't have anybody, then."

"You did, but you didn't want us. Other than Harry."

"What about the third time?"

"That was one of the easier ones. You were willing to watch the videos. It was only a few days after the reset."

"Oh. That's fast." She looked down at her lap. "I guess

we've done all the other stuff. The sleeping in the bed stuff."

So, she was figuring things out. I figured *Cosmopolitan* would fill in anything she hadn't picked up from TV shows. "We did. There's a lot to it if you haven't looked it up."

"Oh, I've been on the internet," she said. "You can't Google much of anything without encountering naked people."

I choked on my laugh. "You can use a safe search."

"Oh no, it's very interesting. I had no idea boobs were so many different sizes."

I coughed into my hand. "Um, yeah. Male parts, too."

"Really?" Her head pops up. "Is that why people keep saying 'size matters' all the time?"

"Yeah."

"What does it matter *for*?"

Sex ed. Not my strength. "Um, some women like men to have bigger parts. They think it is important to like what men do with it."

I winced at my awkwardness. Maybe one of these days I'd rehearse the right ways to manage these conversations. I'd loved Ava since I was seventeen, and we had been together hundreds of times. But this was a new Ava. I had to treat her carefully.

"I should probably write these things down so that next time this happens, I know what I like," she said.

"You might have already," I said. "I only know the things that are in your book. But you may have notes I haven't seen."

"I don't think so," she said. "I've been through this house pretty thoroughly."

"Well, I know what you like," I said. "I've memorized every part of you."

Her blue eyes searched mine. I remembered the first time she looked up in the hospital room and I saw that startling color. It broke my heart that our history was erased for her. All those intimate acts. Those nights and days and words. Lost to her.

At least I still had them. And we'd documented what we could.

She sat up. "We could video ourselves doing it. Then I'd know next time what we've done."

I choked again. "That might not be advisable."

"Why? I have the camera."

"Things like that can get out, be seen by other people."

Her mouth made an O, her eyes wide. "Then I guess pictures are a bad idea, too."

"Probably."

"People do that, though, right? I mean, it's all over the internet."

"Totally. Some people make their living selling videos and pictures of, uh, you know, *that*."

Her eyes got big again. "Really? They get money for it?"

"They do."

She sat back against the cushions. "Huh!"

"I'm not sure it would be a good lifestyle fit for us," I said carefully.

She nodded. "I get it. Future Ava might not like that past Ava flashed her cootchie all over the internet."

She was picking up slang. It was funny to hear it coming from her. She settled back against me. "So, what do I like?" she asked, her voice whisper-quiet.

I knew what she was asking. "It shifts according to

your mood," I say, "but after a romantic movie, you like to kiss Hollywood style."

"How is that different?"

"You want me to describe it, or show you?"

"Show me, I think."

She squished her eyes closed and leaned forward.

I had to smile. She looked like she was expecting a tetanus shot. Instead of kissing her right away, I touched her hair, gently tucking a strand behind her ear. I ran my thumb along her cheek and down her jaw, then cupped her face.

I waited until her shoulders relaxed, and her features were no longer in this pained expression. Then, and only then, did I actually lean forward and softly press my lips to hers.

We'd been kissing for weeks, but they had been gentle and easy, like middle school kisses.

Now, I gripped her chin more firmly. I slid my tongue against her lips, teasing them open.

She parted, our mouths fully engaged, and I drew her tightly against me. My fingers slid through her loose hair to hold the back of her head.

Her body melted against mine. I let go of her chin to drag her from the cushion beside me onto my lap. She turned to face me, knees on either side of my waist, her legs on either side of my thighs.

I released her head to spread my hands across her waist and then down to drag her even closer.

She gasped against my mouth. "Tucker, I feel like I'm on fire. Is this normal?"

"Totally," I told her. "Do you want to stop?"

"God, no," she said. "I think you better show me what happens next!"

So, I did.

CHAPTER 24

Ava

After three solid days in bed where Tucker and I called in sick to everything, we finally felt ready to go out into the world again.

I swear, everything looked different. I saw love everywhere. Old couples, young couples, people on first dates. I could spot the people who were clearly doing all these crazy things with each other and liked it. And I could even figure out when one person liked it more than the other.

It was all in the gaze, the way their bodies shifted toward each other or away. How comfortable they were touching.

Tucker and I had it now.

I wanted my whole life back. All of it.

We started making expeditions to places around town so I could practice with my camera. Austin was so big!

We went to the State Capitol building to photograph the towering trees and intricate architecture. We spent sunset under the Congress Street bridge waiting for the bat colony to fly into the sky to begin their nightly scavenging for food.

Graffiti murals. Kayaking on the lake. Bull Creek Park.

I started taking more photos of people, handling all the families with small children that Vinnie was relieved I could do. I figured out Photoshop and increased my time at my computer.

I only rarely worked shifts at Big Harry's.

The photos I took began to look like the ones from before. I made more money and worried less.

Tucker moved back into our blue house.

I met Maya, hanging out on her flower-filled porch next to the one where I'd lived with my mother, where Tucker would sneak me out the window when we were teens.

When I got my license back, we drove to Houston for weekends with my father and Tina and my half sisters.

We added to my scrapbook, new photos and stories. I thought hard about what would work to get my attention if this happened again. I left the warnings about my mother, but made sure Tucker was represented early and often in the pages.

Maybe getting my life back would simply always be hard no matter what we did. But I wanted to shore everything up while the feeling of loss and fear were still close, to remember what helped me and what didn't.

I hadn't been to Mount Bonnell, even though I'd seen photos from there in my old albums.

As Thanksgiving approached, Tucker suggested we have a picnic at the top of the massive staircase that overlooked the river snaking through the city.

"This is a lot of exercise," I huffed as we climbed the stone steps.

"One hundred and six stairs," Tucker said. "You used to practically run up them."

"Really?" My thighs ached. I guessed old Ava was more active. "A person could go right into a seizure from this level of exertion."

That stopped Tucker cold. "Maybe we shouldn't go up."

"No, no." I passed him on his step. "Have I ever had a seizure from working out?"

"No." He hurried to catch up.

"There you go. Did I used to jog or something?" Dang, this was hard.

"No. You rushed around more. I think you'll feel more in shape when you do more outdoor shoots."

That made sense.

When we made it to the top, several people stood by a stone wall. We approached it as well.

Down below, houses clustered into neighborhoods. The water sparkled as it wound its way through. Homes way fancier than ours stood on the shore, jutting out with perfectly manicured lawns, and, inexplicably, swimming pools.

"Why do they have pools when the lake is right there?" I asked Tucker.

"Beats me. I've never been a rich person." Tucker took my hand. "Come on."

We went off to the left of the overlook and walked down a rocky trail through the brush.

"Where are we going?" I asked.

"Here," he said. A small clearing had a concrete table and benches. "For our picnic."

He shrugged off the backpack and unloaded containers of fruit and potato salad and ham and cheese sandwiches.

The water bottles were icy from being partially frozen.

I stood on top of the table so I could see the city. "It's a different view from here."

"We can walk along the other side after we eat. There are lots of great spots for photographs."

"Oh!" I had totally forgotten I had my camera, overwhelmed by the view.

We sat on the table while we ate so we could see above the scrubby brush. The wind was high up here, sending my hair flying. I tucked it into the collar of my sweatshirt.

"Why does the food taste so much better here?" I asked Tucker, having gobbled my sandwich and a good portion of the potato salad.

"The exercise, I think," he said. "Maybe the great outdoors whets your appetite."

I stood on the table again, this time with my camera. "I feel like I could take a thousand photos and never capture what it's like to be up here."

He stuffed the leftovers into his pack and climbed up beside me as I snapped shot after shot. "There are some things we can't capture with images alone, not even video with sound."

"The wind whipping your hair," I said.

"The smell of dust and green."

I elbowed him. "Green doesn't have a smell."

"Doesn't it?"

I sniffed. "Okay, maybe it does."

When I felt I had taken all the shots I could, we jumped down. This time, when we returned to the stone wall, it was empty. I photographed more of the view, zooming in on the details I'd missed. A small boat motoring along the surface of the lake. A bird nest almost hidden in the branches of a tree below.

We wandered down a broad path of gravel and dirt, with boulders bordering the edge.

Here, there was no wall or brush to keep you from tumbling over the edge. My fear spiked, but I pushed it back down. I knew how to be careful. I didn't have to be afraid.

"Where does this path go?" I asked.

"Back to the road where we parked," Tucker said.

"You mean we didn't have to walk up all those stairs?"

He laughed. "One time we came up here, we took the path, and you complained that the stairs would have been faster."

"I guess you can't win."

He took my hand. "Coming here with you is always a win."

We spotted a big flat boulder and sat down, looking over a new portion of the lake. "I love this city," Tucker said. "I'm glad this is where I was born."

"Me, too," I said. "I'm glad Dad didn't take me away to Houston. That city has its good points, but it mostly smells like car exhaust."

Tucker grinned and squeezed my fingers. "I love how you describe things."

I sighed. "I still talk a little weird. Sometimes I don't catch it until after I hear my own words."

He lifted my hand to kiss the back of it. "It's perfect. And I don't think I've said it in a while because it seemed like you didn't want to hear it, but I love you, Ava. I didn't stop loving you at any point in all this."

His soft gaze was already familiar. I'd captured this expression on him a hundred times. Based on the sheer volume of the printed images, it was always my favorite.

I leaned over to bump his shoulder. "I think I love you,

too, as much as I can tell what love is. *Cosmopolitan* isn't a very good source for relationship advice, it turns out."

He laughed at that. "It's fun to read, though."

"Movies aren't good either," I said. "It's like they meet, they montage through a bunch of dates, and then, bam, they're in love."

"I think David and Patrick are a good example," he said. "They took their time. They had problems. They had great moments."

"Like when David sang to him."

"Just like that."

"But remember when Alexis and Ted had to say good-bye? That was so painful."

He wrapped my hand in both of his. "We won't ever have to do that. I will go wherever you go."

"But you're in school! You have a job."

He shook his head. "Those things don't matter."

"You *do* love me, don't you?"

He leaned in to brush his lips on mine. "One thousand times over." Then he pulled away to tug a box from his pocket. He placed it in my hand.

By now, I knew what a small velvet box meant. I opened it, and a diamond ring sat inside. I recognized it, too. I'd worn it in lots of pictures before our wedding day. The only reason I hadn't had it on me in the limo was that it had been passed to Tucker's friend Bill to hold until the right moment in the ceremony.

"Are you ready to wear it again yet?" he asked. "Because I still want more than anything for you to be my wife. I've weathered all this many times, and I will do it as many times as I need."

I stared at the gemstone sparkling in the sun. My throat caught. Could I do this?

I didn't answer him right away. I was so unsure. It wasn't that I doubted how he felt about me. And I recognized this connection to him that I was sure related to all the times I'd loved him before.

But survival Ava was unpredictable. It wasn't something I could control.

And even more importantly, I realized something critical after taking all the photographs over the last few months. Marriage often led to children.

Tucker only had his Gram. Surely, he'd want to create a family of his own.

There was no way I could do that. I wished old Ava had written something down about this. Had she thought this through when she agreed to marry Tucker before?

Or was the old version of me willing to have a family? I wasn't now. When I watched those tiny, vulnerable humans turning to their mothers when they bumped their knee or got scared by a stranger, I knew I could never be responsible for something so fragile, so tender.

What kind of mother could I be if I forgot my own child? If I had a seizure in the living room, and they came to me, and I screamed for them to get out? Or worse, I was in a grocery store and took off, leaving them in a shopping cart because I didn't know they were mine?

The horrifying scenarios lined up. Leaving them in a park or in some dangerous place like a hot car, strapped to their seat.

Even if we were at home, I could forget them in a bath or alone in a high chair, running from the house as I panicked about who I was.

I shivered. No. Never.

To be married to me would mean to never have kids.

And Tucker would be such a great dad. I couldn't take

that away from him. He would say it didn't matter. That he loved me more than those hypothetical children.

Even so, we needed to have that conversation before I could agree to marriage. Maybe I could ask my dad or Big Harry if I had ever brought it up to them.

But I couldn't tell him yes or no. I wasn't ready to do that right now.

I closed the box and stuck it in my pocket.

"Can I answer that later?" I asked him. "I'm still not quite comfortable in this skin yet."

He drew me close. "Of course. Absolutely. I only wanted to make sure you knew where I stood."

I leaned my head on his shoulder. I loved him. I absolutely did.

But truthfully, I was only five months old. I couldn't make a decision like this.

Not yet.

CHAPTER 25

Tucker

December was a whirlwind. We taught Ava our Thanksgiving traditions, a mix of Gram's and her father's. As we rolled into the Christmas season, Ava and Vinnie were slammed with family photos.

And I was finally graduating with an associate's degree in supply chain logistics. With so many manufacturers in Austin, it felt like a safe, easy career path to support Ava.

The morning of graduation was laid back, nothing like the wedding or even high school. Marcus came down, which was nice, plus Gram and Harry and Maya.

Ava and Vinnie both took photos, although Vinnie insisted that when it was time for me to walk across the stage, she needed to enjoy the moment and let him do the snapping.

I knew she'd never do that.

And sure enough, when I glanced out at the seats after they called my name. I spotted her hair around the camera lens. Gram and the others whooped it up.

I turned in time to shake some random administrator's hand and take my empty diploma case. Life would get easier without classes on top of everything else, even though I'd only been taking one or two courses a semester.

I had three interviews lined up in early January, part of the recruitment set up by the college.

Ava and I weren't kids anymore, not by any definition. She had her photography degree. I had mine. Real jobs. Real lives.

If only she'd agree to marry me. I didn't know how or when to broach the subject again. The legal standing would make me feel more secure that I could handle anything her condition sent my way.

After the caps filled the air and made their pointy descent on the crowd, I pushed through the throng to my little group. It was easy to spot Big Harry. He towered over everyone, especially my diminutive Gram.

Ava threw her arms around my neck. "You did it! You're all done!"

Marcus shook my hand. Maya and Gram hugged me from either side.

"I thought we could head out to the Oasis for dinner," Marcus said. "We should get there in time for sunset."

"How lovely," Gram said. "I don't think I've been there since Tucker's grandfather was alive."

When everyone was still alive. I remembered that dinner. Stephen was in kindergarten. I was a second grader. We'd annoyed the more serious diners by running along the decks.

"What's the Oasis?" Ava asked.

I unzipped my graduation gown. "A huge restaurant overlooking Lake Travis. It's known for its sunset views."

Gram took my diploma and cap. "The food is all right, but it's definitely a destination spot in Austin. It will be delightful."

Marcus drove Harry and Maya out while I took Ava, Vinnie, and Gram. I was surprised when we arrived to find Bill and his new girlfriend Samantha, as well as Fuentes and some woman I'd never met.

"I invited your friends," Gram said.

"That's great, Gram." I shook Bill's hand. "Glad you came.

"Congrats, you slowpoke," he said, his arm around Samantha. "About time you got out of there."

Fuentes clapped me on the back. "My man. Now, you're too good for Jiffy Lube." He dragged his arm around a woman in a tiny, low-cut red dress. "This is Diana."

The woman clung to his arm, eyes on Fuentes. "Congrats."

"Thanks." I took Ava's hand. "Let's head in."

Ava was quieter than usual as we took up a large table on one of the many decks of the restaurant. Fuentes was the loud one, regaling everyone with stories from the garage, cars we'd worked on, problem customers. Half of them were made up, but he was entertaining.

Vinnie took pictures. Marcus kept the appetizers coming.

As the sun set, I walked Ava over to one of the balconies.

She exhaled slowly, leaning over the rail as if to escape everyone. "It's a lot of people. I forget how hard that can be. Was I always like this?"

"More or less. I didn't realize we were coming here. I might have suggested something smaller."

"No, it's pretty. And you know how Dad is when he gets an idea in his head."

"Like father, like daughter."

She huffs a laugh. "I might be a little peopled out."

"We can run away."

She laughs. "Think I can make it to the water from here if I jumped?"

"I'm not sure you can swim."

"Really?" Her eyebrows drew together. "I guess we haven't tried that, have we?"

"Pools and lakes aren't something we've done. Seizures and swimming aren't a great combination. But we can try it."

She shrugged. "I should probably find out. For safety reasons. Add it to the scrapbook."

"We should." I leaned my elbows on the rail. Strings of colored lights blinked on as the light faded. "You didn't bring your camera."

"Vinnie is more into sunsets than I am. I do like photographing the water, though."

I didn't mean to ask the next question, but it tumbled out. "If I get one of the industry jobs in the new year, will you consider marriage? You'll get kicked off your dad's health insurance when you're twenty-six in June, and you could get on mine if we're married."

"Ah, a practical proposal." She stared out at the darkening water. "Let's not talk about it tonight, okay? It's your big day."

My stomach fell. "Okay. I won't push. We'll figure out the health insurance piece."

She nodded. "Dad has been looking on the exchange."

Of course, he was.

Vinnie approached. "Turn around, let's get that last bit of light with the hotshot grad."

We smiled for the picture, but I wasn't feeling it. I was hoping to make some progress with Ava.

But I'd have to be patient. Six months had passed since our failed wedding. We were as close as ever, otherwise. Things were good.

Even so, something was holding her back. If she didn't want to talk about it, I would simply have to wait.

CHAPTER 26

Ava

I was peeing red.

I stared at the toilet paper, aghast. What was going on?

I'd been feeling off all day, my belly cramping like I'd eaten something bad.

And now this.

We were supposed to be on our way to Houston for Christmas Eve with my dad. We were spending the night there, then coming back on Christmas Day to have dinner with Gram and Big Harry. Maya was in Chicago visiting her nephew and his wife.

I wiped it up again, but more kept coming out. I wasn't peeing anymore, but the red kept coming.

What in the world?

I pressed the toilet paper to my body as I scooted toward the counter to grab my phone. When I was safely seated again, I Googled, "Red urine."

That was alarming. Urinary tract infection. Kidney infection. Kidney stones.

Except I didn't have any of the other symptoms.

I tried a different search.

"Red coming out of body."

That was worse. Anal fissures. Was it coming out of my butt?

I checked.

Nope.

But it was thicker now. Wait. Was this blood?

And it was coming out more toward the front. And some of it was stringy.

Another cramp seized me. What the hell?

I tried another Google.

"Stringy blood and cramps."

I read only a few lines and realized this was a period. Of course, it was. Flo at the diner used to complain about them all the time, her situation made even worse because people sometimes called menstrual cycles "Aunt Flo."

This should have been happening once a month. Why hadn't it been? And why was it coming now?

I scanned more information. Pregnancy stopped cycles. But I hadn't had one since my memory reset, even in the months before Tucker and I were back together.

I peered into the bowl. It wasn't coming fast. Maybe it wouldn't be too bad.

I Googled what to do. Insert a tampon, a menstrual cup, or use a pad. I rolled up a pile of toilet paper and trapped it in my panties, then searched all the cabinets in the bathroom even though I was pretty sure I wouldn't find any of those things.

And I was right. Nothing.

So, this hadn't happened to me before? Not ever? Why not?

A knock on the door startled me. "Ava, are you okay?"

"Yes!" I called. God. I should tell Tucker.

But something about this embarrassed me deeply.

Why? It was just a period. Maybe it was the way Flo had talked about it. Or the tone of the articles I'd read. This was something you kept to yourself. Something private.

I'd keep reading in the car. I could stop at a store on the way to Houston and buy what I needed.

After checking to make sure the toilet paper wad was handling the mess, I pulled up my black dress pants and washed my hands. Another cramp hit. Gah. Being female sucked.

Tucker waited in the hall, holding a laundry basket full of gifts. "Everything all right?"

"Yeah. Just bathroom stuff."

I frantically studied my options in the car as we drove through town. Tampons sounded difficult and invasive. Menstrual cups, too. I decided that pads with wings would work for today until I had time to figure out how to handle the other things.

"Can we stop at that CVS?" I asked as we approached the freeway.

"Sure. You forget something?"

"Yeah." I decided saying less was more.

He pulled into the parking lot.

"I'll run in." I lunged out of the car.

The glass door slid open as I passed through.

"We close in fifteen minutes for the holiday," an employee called as I walked inside.

"Okay. Thanks."

I'd better make this snappy.

I realized for the first time what the "feminine hygiene" aisle referred to. This. Periods. Bleeding. I'd passed it dozens of times and never bothered to look.

The shelves had too many options. But I found something for medium flow, with wings, and snatched it up.

Then I hesitated. I had to buy it first. But that put me by the front door. Then I'd have to go deep into the store to find a bathroom. That might be weird.

Shoot.

I was the only one here besides the lone cashier, who leaned on the checkout counter, staring out into the empty parking lot.

The bathroom sign hovered over a short hallway. I couldn't take the box in there. She'd think I was stealing it.

What to do?

Finally, I opened the box, extracted one pad, and carried both to the hallway. I left the box on a shelf nearby and went inside.

At least this part was simple. I dropped the icky wad of toilet paper into the toilet and pulled the strip off the adhesive. It went inside my underwear easily.

That wasn't so bad.

I flushed and washed my hands again, staring at myself in the overbright lights.

So, this was womanhood. Weird it was so delayed. Maybe because of my condition? Maybe this was my first time. I had no idea. There were no notes in my scrapbook about this.

Time was ticking. I hurried out of the bathroom. The open box waited on the shelf. I picked it up to take it to the front. On a whim, I grabbed a box of candy canes as I approached the counter.

The cashier checked out both items. "Eight ninety-five."

I paid with a card while she dropped both things in a bag. Perfect. It wouldn't be obvious.

Tucker waited in the car. "Got what you needed?"

I broke the plastic on the front of the candy cane box

and pulled out a pair of them, passing him one. "For the road."

"Nice." He took the candy. "Let's go be merry."

I bit off a piece of mine while I continued to Google. Sure enough, seizures plus the medications for seizures could make periods erratic and delayed. Now I knew.

I was fine. I'd bring it up with my doctor when I went next time. In the meantime, pads would handle it for the next five to seven days.

I shut off the phone and cranked up "Jingle Bells" on the radio. I was relearning the common holiday songs. No need to dwell on bodily functions when it was my very first Christmas. I was glad it happened at home, and it was so easily handled.

Tucker and I sang the whole way.

CHAPTER 27

Tucker

I put the wedding talk completely behind me as Ava and I moved into a new year. I got two job offers and accepted one, putting me into the nine-to-five class I'd never experienced.

Was this what it had been like for my dad, leaving every morning to fight traffic to work, being gone all day, then fighting it back home?

I saw Ava less because she and Vinnie often scheduled photo shoots for the golden hour, so she missed dinner.

But we had weekends, when there weren't wedding gigs, and our evenings.

In February, I took the day off for both Ava's and my neurologist visits. We were seeing the same doctor and had scheduled ours back to back.

Dr. Simmons ran us both through the usual eye tracking and muscle tests. "You both seem good. Any concerns?"

"None here," I told him. "Although my VNS is over six years old. They said seven to ten years on the battery."

"Do you manually stimulate it a lot?" he asked.

"Not really."

"I'll put in for the technician to test it at your next visit," he said. "It's a simple connection between a wand and a monitor. It will tell us when you might need to replace it."

"Which is surgery, right?" I asked.

"Yes, but very minor compared to the original one. We don't have to touch the wire, just the device."

"Okay, cool." I stepped back so Ava could talk to him.

She hesitated for a moment, and for a second, I wondered if I should leave. But then she said, "I was curious about my menstrual cycle."

"Oh?" Dr. Simmons looked up. "Your OB/GYN should be able to guide you on that."

"Yes, I guess, but I read that seizures and the medication could delay them?"

He frowned. "I suppose they can, in theory, although that would more likely be for young teens, and the medication you are on doesn't have that side effect. Nor do you have the frequency of seizures where we see other body impairments."

She sat up. "Oh. So, you're saying my cycle shouldn't be affected?"

"I wouldn't think so. Besides, it says here you've always taken Depo-Provera as a precaution in case your seizures were hormone related. That would be the reason your cycle has ceased."

Oh, God. Her shots. All the blood ran from my face. "Ava, we haven't gotten you in for a shot since the last seizure."

She turned to me. "Should we have?"

"They're only good for three months."

Her eyes got wide. "It's been eight."

"Okay," Dr. Simmons said. "I would check for pregnancy. You could certainly go from the shot to a pregnancy without ever having a cycle."

"I had one a little over a month ago," Ava said. She pressed her hands to her cheeks. "Christmas Eve."

So, that was why she stopped on the way to her father's. And why she was elusive for a few days. Why hadn't she felt she could tell me? We could have handled this. And I would have remembered the shot. Not that I ever had much to do with it. The OB/GYN visits weren't ones I typically went to. But, of course, she hadn't been.

"Let's stay on top of this," Dr. Simmons said. "Because the current drug you are on has not been sufficiently tested for safety during pregnancy. We'll need to switch you."

"I'm sure it's nothing," Ava said. "I haven't been sick or tired or anything." She smiled, but I could tell she was masking her anxiety.

"Okay, good. But do let us know." He stood from his stool. "Otherwise, I'll see you in six months. Tucker, we'll test that battery then."

"Great, thank you."

When he left, I turned to Ava. "Christmas Eve, right?"

She nodded.

"That would have been the last week of December." I counted on my fingers. "Then four weeks of January and a week of February. You should have had another one by now."

"I know."

"Let's stop at the store on the way home. We have to know right away."

I wanted to kick myself the entire drive to our neighborhood. Why hadn't I checked on something so important? I guess because I'd never had to.

But if she bled in December, she wasn't pregnant then.

And probably she was only late because it had been years since her last cycle. Her mother had put her on the shot as a teen. She might not have had a cycle in a decade.

I tried to relax. The likelihood that she would get pregnant on her first cycle ever was practically nil.

It would be okay.

This time, Ava sat in the car while I ran inside to buy the test. I had no idea which one to get. There was a package with two. That seemed like a good idea. The indicator was very clear, either "Pregnant" or "Not Pregnant."

I stood in line, ignoring the far-too-interested look of the young female cashier. I guessed men didn't buy pregnancy tests very often.

We were quiet on the drive home. Ava pulled the instructions out of the package. "I have to pee on the end of the stick, and then it has a countdown to tell us when the results are ready."

"How long does that take?"

"One to three minutes."

One to three. How quickly a little stick could change the course of your life.

We entered the front door, not talking or holding hands. Every step felt grave, like we were walking into the unknown.

She couldn't be pregnant. Surely not. The world wouldn't do that to us. She would have to change medications. It might not work. We'd reset with a baby in her, not married.

My stomach roiled. I'd let this happen. I was the keeper of the memories, the medication, the appointments.

She'd had her last shot a week before the wedding. I remembered that now. When the next shot came due, she might have gotten a notification and ignored it. We got so much random stuff all the time. Everyone did.

"I'm going to go pee on it," Ava said. She took off alone. I wondered if she would do all of it without me, including waiting for the result. She could be so private. It was more pronounced this time than after any of the other resets.

It was that same hesitation that made her not want to get married, I feared. Something she saw or learned early in this reset had triggered that feeling. She wasn't as close to Maya this time, either.

Maybe it was Harry, or *Schitt's Creek*, or the history documentaries, or working at the diner. Something Flo said. *Cosmopolitan.* We couldn't control what influenced her early thoughts.

It didn't matter now. We could only move forward from here.

She returned to the living room quickly and set the test on the coffee table. It was in countdown mode.

I let out a small sigh of relief that we was including me. She sat down, and I took her hand.

All we could do was wait.

The rectangles at the bottom of the window blinked. There were two when she put it down, then three. Space for one more rectangle remained.

"It will be all right." Ava kept her eyes on the test. "No matter what. It will be all right."

I gripped her hand more tightly. "It will."

Fourth rectangle. It blinked for only a moment before all of them disappeared, and words formed at the top of the window.

I blinked, not sure I could register what it said.

But it was there.

Pregnant.

Ava let out a sob, then jumped up and took off down the hall.

I picked up the test as if somehow the "Not" could show in front, but the single word remained. I set it down again and hurried after Ava.

She had flung herself diagonally across the bed, her face buried in a pillow. I circled the mattress and kneeled next to her, my hand in her hair.

"We'll be all right."

Her shoulders shook. I stroked her head, waiting it out.

All the scenarios lined up. Best case, the new med would work well, no seizures, and then…a baby.

We'd need help if she was going to keep doing photographs. We hadn't changed our lifestyle, and I made more money. We could hire someone for the shooting hours. She could do the digital retouching when I was home.

We'd make it work.

Her voice emerged from the muffling of the pillow. "I'll forget it. I'll leave it in the car. Or at the store. Or in the bath. There will never be a mother worse than me."

I kicked off my shoes and climbed onto the bed beside her. "There is no wrestling that award from your own mother," I said.

She turned her red, tear-strewn face to me. "That's funny, actually."

I drew her close. "I'm here, Ava. You're not facing this alone."

She curled into my chest. "A baby, Tucker. What are we going to do with a baby?"

"Love it?"

"What if it has epilepsy, too? It's like the *Time Traveler's*

Wife. She ends up with the traveling husband and the traveling kid."

"What would Gram say?"

Ava let out a half-sob, half-laugh. "Don't borrow trouble from the future. You've already got enough." She rolled onto her back, sniffling. "I guess we have to make a list. Call Dr. Simmons. Call the OB/GYN. Get the new med." She covered her eyes with her arm. "Prepare for another possible reset."

"We'll make a list."

She lifted her arm to peer at me. "It's your baby, too, isn't it?"

I had to laugh at that. "It is."

"We should get married."

"It might be time. It will help me handle things if…"

"If I forget you and the baby. You can keep the baby even if I run away." She squeezed her eyes closed.

"I don't think that will happen."

"You work all day, Tucker. I'll be alone."

I rolled onto my back next to her. We both stared at the ceiling, thinking.

Then I said, "Maybe we can hire someone full time."

"That's so expensive."

"Gram will help."

She started sobbing again. I pulled her close. "Hey, what about a seizure dog? We could get on a list. You know your dad. He'll find the best company."

"I'll make him pay for it."

I wasn't going to argue with that. God, Marcus was going to freak out when he heard Ava was pregnant. All the better to get married.

Ava sat up. "Let's get married right now. Before the meds change. Before anybody knows anything. We'll keep it a secret until it's done. Then spring it on them in a few weeks."

"Okay."

"Just a few people. Family only." She hopped from the bed and began pacing. "I shot a small wedding up on Mount Bonnell last fall. It was pretty. A small gathering. We like Mount Bonnell. We've been there together."

"We have. We do."

"How fast can we do it?" She lunged for her phone and started typing. "Okay, it says here we can apply at any time. Even today. And we have to wait three days. Then we can do it." She flung her phone onto the bed. "I know lots of officiants. I liked the guy who did the wedding a few weeks ago. He was funny."

I stood next to her. "See, we're figuring it out."

She turned to me, her cheek on my chest. "So, doctors. Wedding. Tell everyone. New meds." She lifted her chin, her gaze meeting mine. "Then what?"

"We hope," I said. "We hope that the seizure stays far, far away."

Her arms wrapped around my waist. "We hope," she repeated. "We hope and hope and hope and hope."

CHAPTER 28

Ava

The OB/GYN got us in the next day for an emergency appointment. The pregnancy was confirmed, and a slew of checkups were scheduled.

Dr. Simmons wanted the med change to happen immediately, so we notified the family that we were getting married that very weekend in four days. We applied for our license, and Vinnie called all over, looking for an officiant who could marry us on short notice.

One of our favorites said yes; he could do a brief ceremony Friday afternoon before a 7 p.m. one that evening. Tucker took off work, and Dad, Tina, and my sisters drove down Friday morning.

I already had a white sundress, and I decided that was good enough. Tucker wore khakis and a pale blue shirt with a tie.

Tina stopped for flowers on the way to Austin and handmade a bouquet plus a matching halo of flowers for my hair and a boutonniere for Tucker.

Harry picked up Maya and Gram. Tucker and I rode

together with Vinnie in the back seat, snapping everything he could.

We didn't take the one hundred and six steps because of Gram, but we slowly made our way up the slope on the back side.

We chose a cluster of flat rocks and waited for the officiant to arrive. It was warm for February, a lovely low sixties and bright sunshine. Harry opened a camp chair for Gram while Vinnie took photos of us.

"This is so romantic," Jennifer said, aiming her phone at herself from an extended arm. "Last minute wedding with my sister!" she said as she took a short video. She made a circle, ending with us in the background.

I shook my head. Everything was a photo op for her.

The overlook was quiet on a February afternoon. Vinnie took pictures of everyone. Gram. Big Harry. My sisters. Dad and Tina. The officiant arrived in a gray suit that almost exactly matched his hair. Vinnie arranged us on the right rocks for the best scenery behind us.

"Let us begin," the officiant said, opening a black folder.

I didn't know if we had written our own vows last time. Tucker rarely spoke of the wedding that never was. But this time, we repeated our lines after the officiant.

The breeze ruffled Tucker's hair. He was happy, his eyes glinting. I did love him. The only thing that had held me back had already happened.

Tomorrow, I would start the new medication and begin weaning the old one. Every day would be like a game of Russian roulette. Would this be the morning my life was wiped again?

I shouldn't think of this now, not with Tucker in front of me, the sun shining down.

I'd seen this moment dozens of times, photographed it for others. I sensed rather than heard Vinnie's camera taking frames.

The officiant asked me to repeat after him. My memory was good enough for this.

"I, Ava Roberts, take Tucker Giddings to be my lawfully wedded husband, to have and to hold, in sickness and health, as long as we both shall live."

Harry passed me the gold band. But I hesitated.

Tucker noticed and tilted his head. "You okay?"

"Why do you love me, Tucker?" I asked. "For a good chunk of our lives, I may not love you. Why do you keep coming back?" I didn't know why I was asking now. It was way too late for doubts. But I wanted to know.

He grasped both of my hands, his gold band clenched between our palms. "Ava, I love every part of you. The fiery side that comes out when you know you need to be strong. The frustrated version when you want to know everything yesterday. The kind part who cares about other people. I don't need you to love me to love you. My love is unconditionally yours because of who you are."

My breath caught. How often did this happen? When did someone love another person like Tucker did me?

I glanced around. Gram was dabbing her eyes. Dad sniffed, his hands clasped tightly in front of his suit jacket. Amanda and Jennifer were a blubbery mess. Even Harry rocked on his heels and cleared his throat.

They believed. This was something big to them.

I reached inside for that voice old Ava always told me to listen to. I was starting to have faith in it. My memories of Tucker were still young, less than a year old. But there were so many. His smiles. His patience. His willingness, actually, his *eagerness* to help, to solve problems, to be what I needed.

I pulled my hands away from him to shift the ring so that I held it between my fingers. "I believe you," I said. "I will always do my very best to come back to you." I looked up at his face, his kind, sweet face haloed in sunlight. "I know you are the one who came to keep me safe."

I slid the ring onto Tucker's finger. For a moment, everything went still, as if nature itself was witnessing this long-delayed moment.

Then, the officiant leaned forward with a broad smile. "Other left."

I laughed and slid the ring off again, transferring it to Tucker's other hand. "It won't be the last thing I get wrong," I said.

"And it won't be the last thing you both laugh about," the officiant said. "Today's mistakes are tomorrow's great stories." He smiled at us both. "Tucker, you may kiss your bride."

As the man stepped aside, Tucker drew me close. I closed my eyes to the bright yellow light, still seeing its golden glow through my lids.

When I felt Tucker's lips on mine, something clicked into place, like the universe had orchestrated this moment. *Do not be afraid,* it seemed to say. *Everything is going to be all right.*

Our small party cheered.

Tucker smiled against my mouth. I couldn't help but grin back. This had been the easiest moment since the day of the pregnancy test. Tomorrow would get scarier, but as each day passed, and the medicine held, it would get better.

We turned to our friends and family.

"We should have a nice dinner," Dad said. "Follow us to Uchi."

I leaned in close to Tucker's ear. "Isn't that a sushi place?" I whispered. "I can't eat sushi with the baby."

He nodded. "How about we go back to the Oasis?" he suggested. "It will be sunset by the end of the meal. It's our happy place."

"Oasis it is!" Dad rubbed his hand together. "I'll give the first toast to this day finally happening."

Tucker had just taken my hand to help me off a rock when a woman stormed toward us in a long cotton dress in the same dusty red as her face.

For a moment, I didn't recognize her. Her hair was cut short. She was overexerted, like she'd run up all one hundred steps.

But then Dad lunged in front of us. Tucker frantically pulled me behind him.

"Ava!" the woman exclaimed.

The strident tone of her voice hit something inside me, and her features connected with the woman who'd followed me that one day, the person in the rose cutting video.

Mother.

"I've got this," Dad said. "I'll throw that witch off the cliff before I let her get her claws on you again." He'd been incensed when we finally admitted she'd approached me in our neighborhood shortly after the last seizure.

He stormed right up to her. "Geneva, you're not welcome here."

She looked around, her eyes falling on Maya. "You're still around?" She swirled around to me. "You invited that old bat before you invited your own mother?"

Marcus leaned in close to her. "You are not invited because you can't be trusted." His voice was even and level.

Her arms flailed as if she could swat away his accusations. Dad stayed menacingly close. He looked like he really might throw her off the cliff.

"I belong here," she said. "I have done nothing but keep her safe."

Dad took another step toward her. They were almost on top of each other. "That's enough, Geneva. This is Ava's wedding day. You don't belong here. I'm ready to call the cops. I renewed the restraining order three months ago when I found out you ambushed her in her own neighborhood."

"As if I was the one who didn't do all the research for her, tried endlessly to find a solution." Mother's face was sweaty and red.

The officiant hooked his arm around my mother's. "Come along," he said. "I'll help you down the stairs."

Mother looked at him, then me, then my father, who held out his cell phone, his thumb on the dial pad.

"I only wanted to see you be a bride," she said. Then she turned and allowed the officiant to escort her away.

Only when Mother had disappeared through the trees, did I feel the force of seeing her thunder through me like I'd been struck by lightning.

She wasn't going to give up. What if she took the baby?

I looked down at the tattoo on my arm, perfectly visible in the sleeveless dress.

Trust only this handwriting.

Maybe she couldn't change my scrapbook anymore, but she was still a threat. She felt like she was owed a place in my life.

"I'm pregnant," I blurted. "Don't let her take our baby, even if I forget I have one."

Everyone fell silence. Tucker drew me in close.

"You're what?" Marcus asked.

"She's pregnant," Tucker said. "And tomorrow she has to change her meds to one that is safe for the baby." His voice cracked on the word. "We'll need all of your help as we go through this."

Harry was the first to lunge forward and draw us both into his extra-large embrace. Gram fitted herself against us, then Maya.

Dad seemed dazed for a moment, then he came forward, extending his arms around our little group. Tina, Jennifer, and Amanda piled in.

"It's my fault she found us," Jennifer said, her voice cracking. "I posted the video of where we were. It's the only way she could have known."

Marcus sighed. "We've all got to be on Ava's team. That means protecting her no matter what."

Jennifer sniffed. "Okay."

"We've got you," Big Harry said. "No matter what happens, we will all be here."

I drew a shuddering breath. This was my family. And soon, there would be one more.

I had to have faith in all of us.

CHAPTER 29

Tucker

Ava and I spent the next few weeks calling every organization that trained seizure dogs, getting on their waiting lists.

The dogs were expensive, some of them over twenty thousand dollars. But more critically, the wait times were around three years since the dogs took that long to train.

But Marcus got things done. He found a company that raised police dogs and identified a pup that had been through years of arduous training but failed the final test.

Then he searched until he found a woman who had retired after years of working with service dogs. With a combination of bribery and emotional plea, she was willing to take the beautifully trained, but not quite K-9 level, three-year-old golden retriever and teach her how to recognize a seizure, help Ava safely to the ground or cushion her fall, and use a landline phone with oversized buttons to call for help.

The training took months to complete, but the new medicine kept the seizures away. Sonograms showed the baby was fine and healthy.

Ava continued to take photographs and go about her day. Vinnie stayed with her as much as possible, and Gram and Maya filled in the gaps.

Finally, after six months, we drove to Dallas to pick up our dog, named Rosie.

I reached across the seat to hold Ava's hand. She rested the other one on her belly, showing plenty of bump.

"The phone is all programmed?" Ava asked. She'd been sleeping more than usual the last week and had left that task to me.

"Yes, exactly the way Glenda said. The biggest button is 911. The two smaller ones are my cell phone and your dad's."

She stared out the window. "We've been lucky so far."

"We have. The new meds are working."

But I knew what was on her mind. At least week's neurology checkup, Dr. Simmons said the likelihood of a seizure during labor was low, but the most common trigger was the rapid breathing most women experience.

They discussed whether to aim for a C-section to avoid that scenario all together since the repercussions of a seizure were so intense for us.

But Ava had never had an epidural either or any surgery. It was all pretty damn scary.

"I've never had a dog before," she said.

"Me neither. And we're getting a super dog."

She laughed. "We won't have to worry about house training her, that's for sure."

I glanced over at Ava. She was a picture, her hair brighter and thicker from pregnancy, her face softer and rounder. I hadn't thought she could be more beautiful, but she was.

We pulled up to the sprawling ranch where Glenda

had retired. Cows milled around, mostly keeping to the shade in the August heat.

We'd be staying on site for the weekend so Glenda could work with us, training us how to handle Rosie and letting Rosie get to know Ava.

We bumped over a cattle guard and crunched down the gravel drive to the main house. Before we even killed the engine, a white-haired woman stepped out onto the porch, waving.

"She looks nice enough," Ava said, shoving her door open with a push of her tennis shoe.

Glenda wore a long floral blouse over stretch pants. She had one pair of glasses on her face and a second pair perched on her head.

"Hello, hello!" she called. "You must be Tucker and Ava." She drew Ava into a hug. "Bless you, child. I'm so glad to help."

She took Ava's arm. "Dad, you get the bags. We can't leave Mom out in the heat." She escorted her up the steps.

Huh. Nobody called us "Mom" and "Dad." The words felt foreign, like they belonged to somebody else.

I opened the trunk and extracted the weekend suitcase. Dust swirled around me. The cows seemed too hot to moo. I slammed the lid and headed for the front door. This place was the epitome of Texas, that was for sure.

Glenda's house was all rodeo, all the time. Cowhides were everywhere, draped over the back of the sofa, hanging on the wall, covering the floor. Longhorns, anchored into red velvet brackets, lined the spaces just below the ceiling.

"We've had our favorites over the years," Glenda said, fingering the brown and white hide on the tan leather sofa. "This one was Buttercup. A real sweet gal." She tapped her foot on the rug. "Millie was not quite so nice, but my youngest son, Cal, took a shine to her, so we keep her around."

Ava's eyebrows lifted. She hadn't had a lifetime of exposure to ranch culture. She shifted her feet to avoid stepping on Millie.

"Why don't you rest up in the guest cabin before we introduce you to Rosie?" Glenda waved to follow her through the living room, entering another large space with floor-to-ceiling shelves, multiple sofas, and a gigantic television.

"Wow," Ava said. "This place is bigger than Dad's."

We continued on to a bright kitchen with a long counter lined with stools, two refrigerators, and four ovens.

"We often feed the crew," Glenda said, waving at a woman rolling out dough on the counter. "We'll have dinner here for you as well around six."

"That's very gracious of you," I said, lifting the suitcase rather than rolling it across the spotless, perfectly shined floor.

Glenda led us out the back door. "Oh, no problem at all. Easiest money I've made in a long time. That dog was near perfect when she arrived."

Outside was a wide, deep porch with cushioned swings, rocking chairs, and a chess set prepped and ready on a wood table. A curving flagstone path branched off in multiple directions. One went to a pool, sparkling blue in the sun. Another shot out toward the first of several barns. And the third went to a small rustic cabin of rough-hewn wood.

"This is charming," Ava said, and I suppressed a laugh. Ava never called anything charming.

"My son and his wife stay here when they come to town." Glenda glanced at Ava's belly. "I keep on hoping for a grandbaby. Maybe one of these days."

She tugged on the screen door, which creaked on its springs. Then she pushed the main door open. "Come on in."

Ava entered first. I followed, wondering if we would be treated to more of Glenda's favorite cows.

But this space was sunny and bright with a red sofa and cherry wood furniture. No taxidermy in sight.

"The main bedroom is off to the right," Glenda told me. "There are cold drinks in the fridge, plus some fruit and cheese. Crackers in the pantry, some other snacks. Make yourself at home." She glanced at her watch. "It's coming on two. How about we meet on the back porch of the house at four?"

"That sounds good," Ava said, the droop in her eyes telling me she really did need to lie down. We took her rest seriously, always. She had hired a third shooter for weddings once she hit the six-month mark and only worked the ones she had booked herself. Vinnie and the new girl, Charlotte, photographed the others.

By fall, she'd be phased out of almost all the weddings other than a few that had been booked a year out and had specifically asked for Ava.

Charlotte was also taking the lead in the family shoots. Ava wasn't sure how close to her due date was safe to book or what her life would look like after the baby arrived.

Glenda paused at the door of the cabin. "Do you know what you're having?" Her eyes glinted, like she was trying to savor this moment as if it were her own.

"A boy," I told her. "We're naming him Tad."

"For Theodore?"

"No, just Tad. It's an, uh, old family name." That was easier to say, we'd learned, than the real reason, which was that the second time Ava and I had ever seen each other, she'd forgotten my real name and called me Tad. To save face, I'd been Tad to her for much of the hospital stay when we were in front of the nurses and social workers.

"That's nice. See you in a couple of hours." Glenda headed out into the sunshine.

Ava led the way to the bedroom. It was homey, with a big blocky quilt that matched the curtains. Ava kicked off her shoes as she walked, collapsing onto the surface like she'd worked all day.

"Why is simply riding in a car so exhausting?" She pulled a pillow under her head.

I lifted the suitcase onto a bench by the window. "It's uncomfortable. You can't move around."

"Mmmm. Wake me at three." She closed her eyes, then opened them again. "Hey."

"Yeah?"

"I got a kick. I real one. Not one of those fluttery things." She pressed her hand to her belly.

I hurried over. I'd had trouble feeling much of anything, even when Ava insisted the baby was kicking. He was too small, and there was too much space.

She grabbed my hand and shifted it near her belly button. "Right here." She held it still. "Wait. Wait. Yes. There!"

A tiny thump pushed against my palm. My eyes instantly felt sharp with tears. "I felt it!"

"He's going at it!" She looked at the bed. "Maybe this firmer mattress has pushed him to one side."

I kept my hand in place as I knocked off my shoes and slid in behind her. Tad was kicking nonstop.

He'd been like a ghost to us at the beginning, only an idea based on the "Pregnant" on the test. He'd become a little more real at the first sonogram, when we could see the lima bean shape of him on a sonogram, one that became more baby-like at five months.

But this. This was his actual foot connecting with my hand. Him. His movement. His way of communicating.

"He's coming, isn't he?" Ava said. "He's going to be here in October."

"He is."

"We should finish the nursery."

We had a crib and a swing and were slowly accumulating clothes from the gifts Marcus and Tina brought to us with every visit. But we had a long way to go moving Ava's office to one side of the room to use the other half as Tad's space.

"We should," I said.

"I won't forget him, will I? How could I possibly do that?" Ava sniffed.

I moved my hand from Tad's kicks and smoothed back her hair. "Some part of him will always be inside you. He will be the first thing you recognize again as yours."

"I hope you're right." She pressed her back against my chest.

I held her tightly as she fell asleep.

We had this conversation all the time. It was something we both had to believe.

CHAPTER 30

Ava

When we pulled up to the blue house after our trip to Dallas, I turned to the back seat. "Rosie! We're home!"

Rosie lifted her red-gold head, her warm brown eyes on me.

I was definitely in love. Both Tucker and I were.

Glenda had shown us all the commands Rosie could do. She would sit and watch your face no matter what commotion was going on. No squirrel, cat, toy, or food could distract her.

She could open the fridge with a pull rope and extract a bottle of water to bring you. She jumped onto tall counters to bring medicine bottles.

When I pretended to fall, she dove beneath me, making sure I didn't hit my head. Then she shoved her nose under my shoulder to roll me to my side, the proper position for someone seizing who might aspirate on their back.

But in addition to her skills, she was a lovable goof. One of the things that got her disqualified from K-9 duty was her incurable urge to lick people's faces. When I sat on the ground, I got nonstop slobbery kisses until I laughed and pushed her nose away.

"Even I can't break her of that," Glenda had said, laughing. "Good thing it's not going to hurt anything."

"It might even make Ava laugh coming out of a seizure," Tucker said. "That might be a good thing."

He was right. I was always so angry and fearful after a reset. Maybe Rosie would be the trick to changing that. She made me giggle in ways I rarely ever felt.

I didn't fool myself into thinking I would never have another memory loss. Life had a way of intervening in our careful routine. Wedding days. Stress. Med changes.

We had prepared for the next one carefully. I had a new scrapbook. I had more videos. All we had to do was add Rosie.

Tucker pulled up into the driveway. "Welcome home, Rosie!"

Rosie pressed her nose to the window, looking out. I watched her from the front seat, wondering what she was thinking. Did she miss her first home? The trainer? Glenda?

"You've been through about as many new starts as I have," I told her. "Let's have some fun."

Tucker opened the back door and unhooked her from the safety harness. I came around the car and took her leash, walking the way Glenda had shown me so Rosie could follow at the right pace and proximity.

"Well, lookie at that!" Our neighbor Isadora walked across the lawn from next door. "You got a dog!"

"Yes, this is Rosie," I told her. "Rosie, sit."

Isadora approached, tugging on the faded T-shirt sprinkled with dirt. She wore the kneepads she used when she gardened and an enormous straw hat. She stripped off her muddy gloves. "Hello, Rosie!"

Rosie sat perfectly still, ignoring Isadora to watch me instead.

"She's a service dog," I said. "For my seizures."

Isadora patted Rosie's head. "Seizures? I didn't realize you had epilepsy, dear." She glanced at my big belly.

It was time to tell the neighbors. My father had said so when we announced the pregnancy. He was right. We needed as many people as possible on our team as we hurtled toward having a baby.

"Yes, I was diagnosed when I was six." I pressed my hand to my belly.

Isadora noticed. "Are you worried about the baby?"

"No, no. Well, of course. I guess it could be inherited, although no one else in my family has it. I guess we got Rosie because we were worried I'd have a medical emergency after the baby comes."

"Oh, my word. You're right." Isadora stuck her gloves between her knees and pulled her cell phone out of her pocket. "I'm so close. I could help with the baby, especially if you need to go to an emergency doctor visit. I raised two of my own, you know. What's your number? I'll text you so you have mine."

I gave her the digits. Tucker set the suitcase inside the front door and came back down the steps. "Hello, Isadora."

"I'm giving Ava my number in case she needs help when the baby comes. She was telling me about the seizures. It sounds so serious."

Tucker's gaze met mine. "Did you tell her about the memory loss?"

I hadn't. I should.

Isadora had stopped typing. "What do you mean, memory loss?"

I reached down to pet Rosie's head. Stroking her soft fur was awfully calming. "When I have a seizure, it wipes out my memory. So, I might not know who you are. I won't know who I am, actually."

Isadora drew in a sharp breath. "My word! What about the baby? You won't remember that either?"

I shook my head. "That's why we have Rosie. She can call for help if something happens."

"Oh, you have to let me know," Isadora said. "I can be here faster than anybody." She quickly tapped out her message.

I turned to Tucker. "I guess we could put her number on the button we were going to use for Dad. That would make more sense. He's so far away."

Tucker nodded. "Good idea. Thank you, Isadora. We'll come around more often. Maybe you and Ted can come over for dinner."

"Oh, no. We should host you. Ava has to be so tired. I remember those days. And I can bring food when the baby arrives. Oh, it's so exciting! I don't have any grandbabies yet."

Everybody sure wanted grandchildren around.

Isadora tucked her phone away right as mine buzzed.

"Thank you, Isadora," I said. "We're going to show Rosie around the house."

"You two take care," she said, reaching for her gloves. "I'll text you for a good night to have dinner."

"Sounds good. Come, Rosie," I said. Rosie fell into step beside me, watching my every move. She really was unmovable.

We followed the instructions Glenda had left for us,

first showing Rosie her automatic food dispenser and water bowl, then the back door, which she easily unlocked and pulled open with the newly installed curved lever and a tug rope.

Then to the refrigerator, where another tug rope was ready for her to open and extract a water bottle.

"Medicine bottle," I told her, tapping a bottle on the counter near the microwave.

Rosie rose onto her hind legs, assessing the situation, and decided she could move the bottle closer and snag it with her mouth rather than jump up.

"Good dog, Rosie!" I said, rubbing her head. "Let's find the telephone."

The new landline was in the living room near the front door. We showed it to her.

"Call 911, Rosie," I said. "Call 911."

Rosie pushed the biggest call button and returned to sit at my feet. We had purposefully left the cord out of the wall so it wouldn't call as we tested.

I sat on the floor. "Call button one," I said. "Call button one."

Rosie raced back to the phone and pushed the smaller button on the bottom right. Then she returned to me.

I held on to both of her soft ears. "What a good dog you are, Rosie. Good dog."

"We should practice you collapsing later," Tucker said. "But right now, you probably really do want to collapse."

He wasn't wrong. "We need to show her the dog bed, and then I'll lie down."

We all walked to the bedroom, where a low trampoline-style bed waited at the end of ours. Rosie recognized it as hers and sat beside it, waiting for our command.

"Go to bed, Rosie," I said. "Go to bed."

Rosie climbed onto the spring surface, shifting the soft blanket around to her liking. Then she lowered her head.

"What a good dog," I said, leaning down to pet her.

"She's going to be the perfect addition to our home," Tucker said.

I couldn't agree more.

CHAPTER 31

Tucker

The countdown to Tad's arrival was particularly nerve-racking for me.

Even with Rosie around, and Isadora checking in on Ava, probably more than Ava wanted, my anxiety was high.

I started having to brace myself when I opened the front door, trying to withstand the terrifying moment between when I announced I was home and when I heard Ava return the greeting.

But the next two months passed uneventfully. Ava moved into more headshot gigs, which she could handle more easily than the families or weddings. Overall, she worked less. Things got a little tighter financially, but we were all right. We were getting by.

Tad was growing at the right rate.

At the eight-month mark, while we waited for Ava's nonstress test to conclude, we spoke to Dr. Chancellor, our OB/GYN, about waiting for labor or to prevent the risk of a huffing-induced seizure Dr. Simmons warned us about.

"We've already labeled the pregnancy high risk due to

her condition," Dr. Chancellor said. "We can easily justify a C-section in her case."

I looked at Ava lying on the exam table with a big strap over her belly. Tad's heart rate squiggled across the screen. "What do you think?"

"I didn't feel great practicing the breathing in birthing class," Ava said. "I'm nervous about it."

"But you've never had a seizure from huffing, right?" Dr. Chancellor asked.

"No. And they made me do it back when I was seventeen. It didn't cause one."

Dr. Chancellor tugged on his stethoscope with both hands. "I wouldn't say you're high risk, but yours is a case where the consequences of a seizure are catastrophic."

We all frowned, imagining a scene where Ava lost her memory mid-labor.

Dr. Chancellor reviewed the screen, then switched off the machine. "Let's schedule it to be safe. Of course, Cesareans have to be performed two weeks ahead of the due date. Once the baby drops into the birth canal, it's much harder to perform one."

"So, the baby would come in two weeks?"

"Or so. The nurse will work on scheduling the surgery. She'll also go over the procedure. I assume you've never had an epidural."

"No," Ava said.

"That shouldn't trigger a seizure either." He patted her arm. "We'll see you through."

"Do you have other pregnant patients with epilepsy?" I asked.

"Yes," he said. "I've had several."

"Did any of them have seizures during labor?"

He hesitated, and at that moment, Ava and I glanced at each other. "Yes. But that was two out of dozens."

I didn't like those odds.

"We'll get it scheduled," Ava said. "We'll be ready."

"Good. I'll see you for one more checkup in a week, then it will be go-time!" He tapped a few things on his iPad as he left the room.

I squeezed Ava's hand. "Two weeks and then he's here."

"I'll have to call Dad once we have a date. I guess we'll know his birthday ahead of time."

"We will."

The nurse popped in. "Let's get you unhooked, and then we will schedule that C-section!"

I held Ava's hand as the nurse worked.

We had made the right decision. Maybe I could worry less about coming home each day.

CHAPTER 32

Ava

The day before the C-section started out in a blur.

I needed to wash the rest of the burp cloths. Clean and air dry the breast pump parts. Fill Rosie's feeder.

Since we had decided Rosie didn't need to go to the hospital, I needed to call Isadora and confirm she had all the instructions for Rosie while we were gone. It would be three days minimum and possibly four because of the surgery.

I moved the burp cloths and the last few baby outfits we'd been given from the washer to the dryer. Rosie trotted along beside me as I moved from task to task.

A darting cramp moved up my belly. I paused, holding my side. The Braxton Hicks contractions didn't alarm me anymore. I'd been dealing with them for days. At my last checkup, Dr. Chancellor confirmed they weren't the real deal. Just the body practicing.

Rosie let out a short, sharp bark. I paused, looking at her. "What?"

She trotted to the refrigerator and opened the door, pulling out a water bottle. She brought it to me.

"Okay, okay. I'll pause for a drink." I returned the water bottle to the door and got a plastic cup to fill from the sink instead. "No microplastics if we can help it, okay?" I took a sip.

Rosie sat at my feet, looking mollified.

"You know you're going to make me pee even more."

Her tail wagged like that was the plan all along.

I looked out the window onto the backyard. Dad had installed a baby swing in the oak tree that shaded the corner. It sat waiting, a bright bit of yellow against the wood fence.

A baby. He was coming. Tomorrow.

I'd gotten a real kick the last few days out of people asking me when I was due and answering, "Oh, in about seventy-six hours." They always looked so confused until I told them that was when my C-section was scheduled.

It was kind of nice being able to know. My bag was completely packed. Extra clothes, nursing bras, mega-panties for the hospital-grade post-partum pads. We even sneaked in my favorite chocolate bars and Tucker's Mountain Dew. Some things were nonnegotiable.

I pressed my hand to my belly. I'd have a wicked scar down low. Dr. Chancellor assured me it wouldn't be noticeable after a few months, but I'd been on the internet. It showed.

I took another sip of water, trying to decide what to do next. Fill the dog feeder for sure, although the bag was full and heavy. Maybe I should have Tucker do it.

Another contraction hit, but this one was like a freight train compared to the others.

I doubled over, dropping the cup. Water slid across the floor like a river.

Rosie's tail stopped wagging. She whined, then

gripped the edge of my sleeve and led me over to the table and chairs.

"Okay, Rosie, I'll sit down." I pulled my arm away, needing it for balance. The contraction had let up, but I still felt like I was being squeezed from within. I kept my breath low and slow. No huffing. Not today.

Braxton Hicks could get more intense than the ones I'd felt so far. I knew this. The difference between them and real ones was that they were erratic rather than regular.

I reached for my phone, which sat across the table, and checked the time.

Three thirty-two.

"I doubt there will even be another one," I told Rosie. That was the way it had been working. They were so far apart that you couldn't even time them. Once a day usually, but maybe one in the morning and one at night.

But I always noted the time, just in case.

Tucker would leave work before too long. Nothing bad would happen, and I'd rather not worry him while he finished up everything he needed to do before taking several weeks off for the baby.

The contraction eased and went away entirely.

"Okay," I told Rosie. "It's over. Dehydration can cause contractions, too, so you were right to make me drink more." I reached down to pet her head. "I should always listen to you."

I surveyed the water on the floor. "I guess I should mop that up. I don't need to be slipping on it."

I lurched back to standing, then waited to make sure the contraction would not return. It didn't. The mop sat in the narrow space between the refrigerator and the wall.

It had fallen toward the back. I snaked my arm toward

the handle, but my belly kept me from leaning in. "Dang it," I told Rosie. "I don't think I can get it."

I pulled my arm out and peered at the mop in the dark corner. The bottom was closer to the front than the top. Did I dare get on my knees and reach for it?

I did a preliminary bend and almost lost my balance.

Nope. Not worth it.

I tugged the dishtowel from the stove handle and dropped it on top of the water. The cup rested on its side. The floor felt a mile away. "Rosie, fetch."

Rosie sat, looking up at me in confusion. I hadn't thrown anything for her to retrieve.

I nudged the cup with my foot. "Fetch, Rosie."

Rosie finally understood, grasping the cup in her mouth and lifting it.

"Good, Rosie!" What a smart dog. I took the cup to move to the sink and dragged the towel along the floor with my foot to soak up the water.

Then it happened again.

My belly clamped down. "Shit!" I cried out, clutching my stomach. I waddle-stepped over to the table to check the time. Three forty-seven. Fifteen minutes. Real contractions started far apart and got closer. This was kind of quick for just two.

I looked at Rosie, who watched my every move. "I'm not even due yet, Rosie," I told her. Maybe I should call Isadora over.

I stabbed at the phone to get to my contacts. This contraction was going on longer and felt deeper.

The urge to huff came over me. No, no. None of that. I drew in a slow breath, and let it out. I started a message to my neighbor. *Can you come ov—*

My belly heaved, and there was no ignoring this one.

My breath sucked in, and a *hoo-hoo-hoo* sound came out of me. It was happening on its own.

I had to stop it. I focused all my attention on my breath. *Come on, Ava, low and slow.*

I reached for the phone to finish the message. I shouldn't be alone, fake labor or not.

But my hand landed on the screen at an awkward angle. The phone slid to the edge of the table and fell.

Something was wrong. I looked at my hand. It wouldn't do what I told it.

I turned to Rosie, but she was already at my feet, whining, tugging at my pant leg to get out of the chair.

I tried to tell her I needed to finish my message, or maybe she should call Tucker. My brain was saying, "Button two." But my mouth didn't work.

I tilted out of the chair. I couldn't stop my forward motion toward the ground.

My face hit the table on the way down, stunning me for a second.

Rosie moved beneath me, and I landed on her soft body.

She wriggled slowly until I was lying on the floor. Now I wanted to tell her to call 911, but no words would come out.

It didn't matter. She knew. She tore off down the hall.

She would call. Call someone.

But it would be too late. My vision was going black. It was happening.

A tear escaped my eye, sharp and hard.

Rosie would make sure I got help.

But even so, everything would be lost.

CHAPTER 33

Tucker

Traffic was lighter when commuting an hour earlier. I had everything arranged for my week off, so I left early. It was the last day I wouldn't be a dad.

My coworkers had given me some gifts during lunch. An outfit or two. A case of diapers. Some toys. It was nice.

We were packed. Ready. This was happening. If we could get through the surgery without any incidents, we'd be home free.

But as I turned onto our street, the bright turn of red and blue lights filled me with dread. Please don't be in front of our house. Please.

But it was.

The yellow ambulance was pulled into the drive.

I parked in front of the neighbor's house and flung myself out of the car.

Isadora stood on our porch, wringing her hands. "Tucker! You're home. Oh, God. It's so terrible."

I didn't even ask her what had happened. I raced inside.

I wasn't sure what to expect. Ava on the floor, seizing. Or getting oxygen, if it were over.

I didn't expect two EMTs to be standing near the end of the sofa.

"What's happening?" I asked, shoving the coffee table aside so I could get closer.

"Do you live here?" one asked, a tall man with a shock of red hair.

"I'm her husband. She's pregnant."

"We can see that. Can you call off the dog?" A woman stood close to Rosie, who I spotted by the arm of the sofa.

"Where's my wife?" I asked.

"Behind the dog," the woman said.

I walked closer. Rosie stood guard, one paw forward in a powerful stance. This must have been from her K-9 training.

"Rosie," I said. "Sit."

Rosie relaxed when she saw me, but she didn't sit.

I approached slowly, extending a fist to Rosie as I got closer.

Then I petted her head.

Rosie whined and turned around to show me Ava.

She was curled in a tight ball, hiding in the space between the sofa and the corner of the wall.

"Ava," I said. "Baby. Come out."

"We think she's in labor," the woman said. "She's had two huffing spells we think are contractions."

Huffing. No. No, no.

I got on my knees. "Ava, can you look up? I'm Tucker, your husband." I reached out to touch her arm.

She yanked it back. "No, no, no." Her face next to her right eye was swollen and purple. She must have fallen.

"I'm here to help you, Ava. We are all here to help."

She peered up at me, tears coursing down her face. "It hurts, it hurts, it hurts."

"Ava, we need to go to the hospital. You're having the baby."

She simply whimpered in her corner.

This was bad. I kept trying. "Ava? Do you know who I am?"

She shook her head.

My stomach clenched. A seizure had wiped her. The huffing caused it. Or something. I know she took her meds. We double and triple checked every morning.

The woman behind me said, "Can you get her out?"

"I'll try. Ava, my name is Tucker. I'm your husband. A man who loves you. Who lives with you."

Ava ignored me, her breath huffing. God, she could have another one if this kept up. It could keep happening and happening.

"Ava, I'm here to help you. So are they." I pointed behind me.

She peered up at them. "Who are those people?"

"They're from the hospital."

"The dog doesn't like them."

"She's trained to protect you. It's okay."

She nodded. "I'm scared. I'm really scared."

"I'm scared, too. Can you come out? We will help make the hurt go away."

The tall EMT stepped forward, making Rosie growl.

"Stay back," I told him. "I can only handle one problem at a time."

"Is she special needs?" the man asked.

I ignored him. "Ava, tell your dog Rosie you're okay so she'll stop guarding you."

Her eyes moved to the golden retriever. "Rosie, I'm okay." Her voice was shaking. "Rosie, move back."

Rosie shifted out of the way as I took Ava's hand and helped her crawl from the space.

I drew her against me. "I'm right here. It's okay. I'll help you. I love you."

She seemed to calm down, pressing her head against my shoulder. At least she was willing to be near me. Feeling her body melt into mine gave me hope that this time wouldn't be so bad.

I let her be for a moment, reveling in this quiet moment. It might be our last one for a long while.

She whimpered. "I don't want the hurt to come back. But it keeps coming back."

"We need to go to the hospital."

She shook her head. "I don't want to."

"It's okay, Ava. We'll get through this. We've done it before, and we will do it again."

"She's had a baby before?" the female EMT asked.

"No," I said. I didn't even want to get started trying to explain the amnesia.

I held her waist as I turned her toward the door. Her pants were soaking wet. She'd never lost bladder control during a seizure. Her water had broken. It really was labor.

As soon as she moved away from me, the EMTs stepped forward to take her.

I hung on to her arm. "Don't do anything sudden. She's been through a lot."

"Sir," the man said. "You need to step aside."

"She needs me," I said. "Stop it."

Rosie sensed the tension and lunged between us and the EMT with a fierce warning bark.

"Sir, get control of your dog!" the woman said.

Shit. I let go of Ava to grasp Rosie's harness. "Rosie, sit," I said. She preferred commands from Ava, but she would take them from me. Ava obviously didn't know them anymore.

While I pulled Rosie back, the EMTs got Ava to lie on the stretcher, then strapped her down.

When Ava realized her arms were locked in place, she panicked. "What's happening? What are you doing?" She writhed on the thin mattress. "Let me go!"

At her panic, Rosie tried to lunge forward. I had to fight her with all my strength to get her down the hall to a bedroom where I could shut her in.

"Rosie, sit," I called through the door.

She was trained well enough not to dig at the floor. From the other room, Ava let out a long, angry scream.

I held back my own panic as I raced to the hall. The EMTs were taking her down the porch stairs.

I wasn't sure what to do first. Get her bag? Lock the door?

Isadora stood where I'd left her, both hands covering her mouth as if she were suppressing a scream of her own.

"We'll need our bag and things eventually," I told her. "And Rosie will need handling. I'm going with Ava. It looks like she's had a seizure and lost her memory."

Isadora reached out with a hand and gripped my arm. "I'm here, Tucker. I'll help. Anything you need." Tears cut through her makeup in muddy rivers. "You go."

I took off across the lawn to climb into the back of the ambulance.

Another contraction had taken over. Ava was no longer screaming, but she whimpered in pain.

I glanced back at Isadora standing on the porch of our blue house. From inside, I could hear Rosie barking.

This was a nightmare.

CHAPTER 34

Ava

I couldn't breathe. The pain was too great.

I kept going in and out of knowing what was happening. My lungs felt pressed from the inside like I was being crushed. I gulped for air, and panic swept over my body as my vision narrowed to gray circles.

"Breathe like this," someone said. I could only make out a form in the haze, but I could hear her fast, hard pants.

"She shouldn't," said a voice. It was the man from the house. The one who had gotten the dog away.

"Stand over there," a firm voice responded. "Stay out of the way. Now, breathe, Ava."

I complied because I didn't know what else to do. I focused only on breathing, and my vision returned. The panic receded.

My clothes were removed and replaced with plain blue fabric like a dress. I shivered from the cold.

The room smelled strong and strange, so different from the house. The bed was narrow with tall sides to keep me in. I grasped the hard plastic with both hands. Squeezing them helped with the pain each time it came.

Strangers surrounded the bed. A woman dressed all in green took a firm grip of my arm. She poked the inside of my elbow with something sharp. I couldn't tolerate any more hurt and jerked away. Blood flowed down my skin in a river of red.

She quickly wiped it with a wet square, which made it sting. "Ava. Be still." Her voice was stern and sent a tremor of fear through me. Who was she, and why was she so cruel?

On the far side of the bed, the man from the house tried to lean in. "Ava, please trust us. I know this is frightening. Let them do their work."

I couldn't cooperate. There was no way for me to simply sit and take it. It hurt too much to be poked. I drew my knees inside the blue dress, trying to roll into a tight ball and protect as much of my body as possible from the onslaught.

But there was no escaping the pain within. It began again, rolling through my middle like a black wave, menacing and terrible. I squeezed my eyes shut, trying to wish it away.

"Think of something good, Ava," someone said. "Something pretty."

I tried to think of anything. The house, the dog, the sofa, the people banging on the door.

There had been flowers. They lined the walkway of the blue house as we left.

They were yellow and fat, waving on their stems.

I try to hold on to the image in my head. The yellow flowers were close to the ground, clustered in a sweep of gold. I wanted to lie in them, to go wherever they were.

The pain passed again.

I opened my eyes. A woman with thick black braids wrapped like a crown leaned in close.

She wore yellow, like the flowers. She was not the one who held my arm and stabbed me. "Ava, my name is Kenisha. What can I do to help you?"

"Make the hurt go away so it won't come back."

She brushed hair out of my face. "I can help with the pain, but we need to put the needle in you. It's called an IV."

"Why do I hurt?"

Kenisha lowered the side of the bed to sit next to me. She smelled like comfort. Like calm. I focused on her yellow shirt and a shiny badge hanging in the center. "The pain is a contraction. It's time for your baby to come, and the contractions are pushing it out."

"What baby?"

Kenisha glanced at the man from the house before she said, "The baby in your belly."

Fear thundered down my body. I stared at my distended stomach. It was large, bigger than the bellies of the other people in the room. When I placed my hands on it, something moved under my skin.

A baby? I understand the word. A tiny human. But I couldn't picture one exactly. It was only a concept, like aliens or dragons.

"We're having a baby, Ava," the man said.

Why had he said *we*? He didn't have a big belly.

"You're in labor, Ava," Kenisha said. "Do you know what that means?"

The pain rolled through me again. A low keening cry came out of my mouth, as if I wasn't in control of my own voice.

"Breathe through it, Ava," Kenisha said, gripping my hand. "Work with the contraction."

I didn't know what she meant. My shoulders shook with frustration. "I want it to stop."

She held my hand while I breathed. Everyone stood around watching me. The woman in green. The man from the house. Another smaller woman with short hair in the back of the room.

Then, it finally stopped. I fell back onto the pillow. I was so tired. Tired of pain. Of fear. Of this confusion. I wanted to sleep. Tears squeezed from my eyes.

"Can you make it stop for good?" I asked her.

"I can. And you can rest." Kenisha held up a tiny glint of silver. "This is the needle. It pokes through your skin. It connects to this bag." She showed me a pouch suspended from a tall pole. "We can't get you an epidural for the pain until we have you hooked up to this."

I didn't understand *epidural*, but I nodded and held out the other arm, the one not already hurt by the lady in green. Kenisha ran a cold cloth over the back of my hand instead of the inside of my elbow. The prick was brief, and soon, the needle was taped to me.

Kenisha tucked a thick white blanket around me. "Does anything hurt?"

"Here." I lifted my hand to the corner of my eye.

Kenisha turned to the man who had stood by the window while she poked me. "You want to explain this bruise on her face?" She sounded mad, like maybe he was the enemy.

He moved toward us, but Kenisha swiftly stepped between him and the bed. "Answer me from over there."

He went still. "She probably hurt it when she fell. I need to talk to her now that she's finally calm."

"I think you need to sit down." Kenisha pointed at the sofa.

"Can I at least make sure she knows who I am? She needs my help."

Kenisha glanced back at me, then over at the man, as if sizing us both up. "If it's your baby, why doesn't she already know?"

He hesitated. "She seems confused and lost."

Kenisha's eyes narrowed. "You can talk to her from over there."

He nodded, his mouth in a frown. "Okay." He sat on a gray cushion with his elbows braced on his knees. He rubbed his hand over his eyes. "Ava, I'm not sure what you understood when we were back at the house. I'm Tucker. I'm your husband. The baby in your belly is our son."

I shook my head. "I don't know you."

His face contorted, his eyebrows drawn together. "Ava, I promise. We're in love. We met almost ten years ago."

"I don't believe you."

He blew out a long breath, as if he were in pain, too. "I understand that you don't remember me. This has happened before."

Kenisha straightened up at that. "What do you mean it's happened before? I need some explanations before I call social services and, quite possibly, the police. I have a woman here, in labor, clearly in distress, with bruises on her face and a fear of other people like nothing I've ever seen."

She looked over her shoulder at the first woman who poked me. "Do you have the ER report? They're sure she doesn't have a concussion?"

The green nurse turned the screen she was holding to

Kenisha. "They checked her out. No head trauma, just the bruise on her face."

"Do we have any records on her?"

Tucker tried to speak, but Kenisha held up a hand. "You wait a minute."

The green nurse said, "She's preregistered. Here's her diagnosis." She ran her fingers across the screen and passed it to Kenisha.

Kenisha turned to me. "You have epilepsy?"

I understood the word. "I don't know," I said.

Kenisha turned to Tucker. "So, she has seizures. I still don't read anything here that explains what I'm seeing."

But before anyone could talk, it happened again. The pain surged. I gripped the side of the bed that was still up. "You said it would stop if you poked me!"

Kenisha passed the screen back to the green nurse. "Honey, we're going to help you." She turned to the man. Tucker. "You stay over there until we sort this out." Then to the other nurse. "Page anesthesiology and anyone available in neurology. Let's get her out of pain so we can assess her properly. It would help a lot if we could figure this out before the baby comes."

I groaned. The pain was too much. I didn't know why there was a baby inside me, or exactly how it was going to come out, but I desperately needed this nightmare to end.

They had promised if they poked me, it would end.

Everyone lied. Everything I knew so far was a lie.

CHAPTER 35

Tucker

This was a disaster. Everything was going wrong.

I stood outside the hospital room while the anesthesiologist gave Ava the epidural. They thought I was the bad guy.

I knew what it looked like. Maybe I could get Dr. Simmons to talk to someone about her condition. Or if Dr. Chancellor would get here for the delivery, he could explain it.

I had to be patient. It would get straightened out. My utmost concern was for Ava. She was operating in pure terror. Of course, she was. The pain had to be terrible. She had no idea what was happening to her.

Surely, the epidural would help.

And I still had to tell everyone. It had been a race since I got home.

I texted Gram first.

Me: Ava is in labor. She had a seizure. Rosie called 911. She's getting an epidural. It's about as bad as you might imagine.

I didn't wait for an answer but moved on to the next. Ava's dad.

Me: Ava went into labor early. She had a seizure. She has no memory. Rosie called 911.

Right as Gram's reply came through, the phone buzzed with a call. Marcus.

"What the hell happened?" His voice boomed so loudly I had to pull the phone away from my ear.

I figured he'd want details. "When I got there, the EMTs had already arrived. She was hiding in the corner."

"What was the dog doing?"

"Standing guard. Rosie called for help like she was supposed to."

"But it still happened!"

He wasn't thinking straight. It wasn't like Rosie could prevent a seizure. "She was huffing pretty hard with the labor pains. It probably hit right away. Looks like she fell. She has a bruise on her face."

"The dog was supposed to prevent that!"

"There's no telling how fast it happened. Look, she's getting an epidural. I need to call Isadora to handle Rosie and bring us our bag."

"You didn't bring the bag?" Every sentence was an accusation.

"Not on the ambulance. And I don't have my car. Look, we're okay. We'll figure this out. We can talk when you get there."

"I'm walking out of the office right now. I'll go straight there."

I didn't point out that he wasn't getting a bag either, and he didn't have an amnesiac wife in labor. "I need to notify everyone."

"I'll call back from the road." He hung up.

I blew out a long breath. This was hard.

I read Gram's message. *Should I come up?*

That was a good idea. She could bring the bag when she did. Better than Isadora going out of her way. But not yet. Things were too wild for visitors.

Me: Yes. I'll let you know when we have a timeline. Right now, they think I hurt her or something. I need to get that handled. I left the bag at home. It's on the dresser. Can you bring it?

Gram. Of course. I'll see to Rosie. You can let me know when I should come up.

Me: We'll need a few more things.

Gram. You can send me a list.

I relaxed a small degree. She could bring the scrapbook. We needed that. Ava hadn't wanted it to get damaged in the duffle bag, so it was in her office. The important videos were on both of our phones.

Ava's phone. We would need to find that, too.

I would explain all this to Gram when we got to that point.

I texted Isadora next.

Me: We're settled. Please let Rosie out of the office if you haven't. Gram is coming to look after her until she comes up here. Thank you. I'll update you.

Isadora: That was so scary. Are you okay? Is Ava okay?

Me: As much as we can be. She's getting an epidural, and we'll go from there.

Isadora: I'll be praying for you both. Baby, too.

Me: Thanks.

Right. The baby. In all this, I was mostly worried about Ava and the dog and her trusting me and getting to the hospital.

But the baby was on the way. Ava just found out she was pregnant.

She didn't even know his name. Had she understood

that I was the father? Did any of this make sense to her at all?

She'd been focused on the pain. She was so afraid.

I leaned against the wall. This was too much, too much.

I had to pull myself together. Ava was in there, lost and confused. I had to get proof of her condition. Get the doctors involved.

But all the doctors' offices were closed now. Maybe they would page Dr. Chancellor. I would have to try if they didn't. He had said that an obstetrician on call would deliver her if he wasn't available.

Another stranger. A doctor who didn't know or understand.

A middle-aged woman in a floral dress approached, her hair swept into a glossy black updo. "Are you Ava's husband?"

I shoved my phone into my pocket. "Yeah."

She held out a hand. "I'm Clarissa, a social worker here at the hospital."

Right. The one who would decide if I had hurt her.

I stood up straight and reached over for a handshake. "Nice to meet you. Ava's getting an epidural."

She nodded. "Could you sit with me for a second?"

I didn't want to. I was ready to get back in the room the moment I was allowed, but maybe I wouldn't be allowed if I didn't pass her test.

"Sure." I followed her down the hall to a section of chairs. They were empty.

"Let me make sure I have the details right," she said.

We went through the basic questions. Names. Address. Birthdates.

"Can you tell me how Ava got the bruises? The nurses are concerned about her condition."

I had to get this right. "Ava has epilepsy. We have a seizure dog at home to help her. My best guess since the EMTs were already there when I got home from work is that she fell when she had the seizure, and Rosie called 911."

"The dog called an ambulance?"

"We have a special service dog phone. Rosie is highly trained."

She used a stylus to take notes on an iPad. "I see. So, you were at work all day?"

"Yes, I left at eight that morning."

"And Ava was alone?"

"She was with Rosie."

More scribbles. "Did she have the bruise when you left that morning?"

What was she talking about? I already told her how she got it.

But I had to be calm. "She did not." I decided to repeat myself. "She most likely got it when she had the seizure."

"How do you know she had a seizure if you weren't there? Did she tell you?"

Now, we would get to the part that was hard to believe. "Because she lost her memory."

"Her memory?"

"Yes, her seizures cause her to lose her memory. That's why it's critical that I get back in there with her."

Clarissa lifted an eyebrow. "Are you afraid of what she might say when you're not in the room?"

What the hell? "No. She can say whatever she wants. I'm worried about her."

"Because she lost her memory." More scribbles.

I should have answered differently. I tried again. "The dog calls 911 if she detects a seizure."

"I see. How often does Ava have these seizures?"

"Rarely. It's been over a year."

"And the dog always catches them?"

"This is the first one since we got her."

"I see." More writing.

I tapped my foot impatiently. "Are we done?"

Her eyebrow lifted again. "I'm here to assess Ava's safety."

Right. "What else do you need to know?"

"Have you ever been accused, arrested, or convicted of domestic violence?"

What kind of question was that? "No."

"Do you have feelings of anger, frustration, or rage that you feel could get out of control?"

"What? No." Other than maybe right now, with her.

She watched me. "How long have you been with Ava?"

"Since we were seventeen. So, uh, eight years."

"And how long have you been married?"

"Eight months."

There went that eyebrow again. "Did you know Ava was pregnant when you got married?"

"Yes, of course. That's why we got married."

More scribbles. "Do you have reason to suspect the child is not yours? Did this make you angry?"

I knew a leading question when I heard one. "Do I need a lawyer?"

She looked up from her tablet. "What makes you think you need a lawyer?"

"This sounds like an accusation. Look, she's my wife. She has a condition almost nobody understands. And she's alone and scared. I need to get back to her."

Clarissa set her tablet on her lap. "Mr. Giddings, if I

don't believe Ava is safe with you, you don't get to see her at all. I call the authorities."

I let out a long, slow breath. This day kept getting worse.

I pulled out my phone. "I'm happy to wait out here. Her neurologist is Dr. Simmons. He's been her neurologist for years and can easily verify her condition and our personal history. Her OB/GYN is Dr. Chancellor. If he comes in, he will also be able to verify everything I've told you."

Clarissa took my phone and tapped the number into her form. "All right, Mr. Giddings. I'll follow up with these physicians. I'll check in with you and Ava in a little while."

I sagged onto the chair. I'd passed.

She got up and swished down the hall. I took a moment to compose myself and headed back to Ava's room.

No one was outside of it. I wasn't sure if I could go in.

I paced on either side for a moment, then knocked.

The nurse in green scrubs who'd had trouble getting Ava to take the IV, opened the door. "We're almost done. I'll come for you."

I hadn't missed anything. As the door closed, I got a glimpse of Ava curled on her side. She must have been between contractions, as she had her head down and didn't seem in distress.

I leaned against the wall again.

We would get through this day. We had to.

CHAPTER 36

Ava

They made Tucker leave when the doctor arrived to put another needle in me, this time in my back.

The cool spray and the pricking sensation were nothing compared to everything else. And when they arranged me in the bed again, the feeling of being crushed inside was gone. All the pain was gone.

"Will the pain come back?" I asked the man who had put the needle in.

"Not until we turn it off," he said.

"Don't ever turn it off," I said.

He laughed with a deep, happy sound. I'd never heard anything like it before.

I smiled at him, then touched my face. For the first time since I woke to the dog licking me, I didn't feel terrified.

Nurse Kenisha told the woman in green that she wasn't sure about Tucker, and the woman in green said, "I called in the dragon. The board gets snippy because she doesn't play by the rules, but she'll suss out if he's a bad apple."

I couldn't follow what she meant. Dragon. Snippy. Suss. Apples. I closed my eyes. Tucker told me he loved me and he was my husband, but those words didn't make me feel anything.

I wanted to sleep.

But not long after that, the tiny nurse let Tucker back in. Kenisha made him sit in the far corner of the room.

The green outfit nurse left, and the small one spread something thick and cold over my fat belly. "I'm Jennifer," she said. "This is for the monitor."

Kenisha came in behind her with a broad strap with a box. "We're going to put this across your stomach. It will tell us how the baby is doing."

Right. The baby. In my belly. The two of them attached it and adjusted the straps.

Jennifer rolled a screen onto a metal table close to the bed. It flickered on, and lines bounced along its surface. "This is the baby's heartbeat," she said. "Do you have a name picked out?"

Tucker spoke up from the corner. "We've named him Tad."

"That's an interesting choice," Jennifer said.

"All right, *Dad*," Kenisha said, emphasizing the word like she didn't want to use it. "Now that we have her settled, can you explain what's going on here? Why is she in such a state? Why doesn't she know she's pregnant?"

Tucker ran his hands through his short sandy hair. It stuck up all over. "Her seizures are a rare kind. They hit her hippocampus, and she loses her memory. I came home, and she was like you see her now. She's not due for two weeks, but her water broke. Maybe that triggered the seizure."

I could only follow some of that. Seizures. Losing memory. Tucker found me in his home. My chest felt more and more tight as he talked. How could this story be true?

Kenisha's voice was still hard. "How often does she have seizures?"

"She hasn't had one for a year and a half. Before we were married. She won't remember our wedding anymore." With that, tears fell from the corners of his eyes. He wiped them away.

I looked back and forth between them. Kenisha watched Tucker, her eyebrows drawn together. "So, Ava doesn't know who you are, who she is, or what is happening?"

He nodded. "When it happens, she can read and write and walk and talk. She's been tested a bunch of times. But anything about her past is gone."

"Good Lord," Kenisha said, tugging her phone from her pocket. "I'll page neurology again."

I didn't know what she meant by that. A page of paper?

She tapped her phone. "Did your OB have an action plan for this?"

Tucker walked forward and gripped the side rail near my feet. "We were doing a C-section tomorrow to avoid the risk of labor."

I tried to follow what they were saying. I knew so little. And I was so tired.

I must have fallen asleep. All I knew was that the bed shifted, and when I looked down, Jennifer was taking away the bottom part and bending my knees up high.

A doctor in blue sat between my legs. He told me to push, but I didn't know what he meant. But there was weird pressure down below. I felt thick where I wasn't thick before.

The pain returned. "You said it wouldn't hurt!" I wailed.

Kenisha gripped my hand. "We need you to be able to feel a few things so you can push the baby out."

Tucker stayed near my head. "Do you want to hold my hand?"

"No," I cried. "I want to go back to sleep!"

The pain came in waves with almost no breaks. I wanted to run away from this awful sensation, push it back up so it wouldn't be down there. Kenisha stayed beside me and told me this was all normal. The baby was coming.

I began to understand about pushing. It was happening even when I didn't try. It wanted the fat feeling to go down and down. I held onto the rails and pushed with it.

Then came a sound like nothing I could have ever imagined. I heard it with my whole body. My belly quivered. My chest tingled. My eyes must have heard it, too, because they started making tears.

"It's a boy," the doctor said and lifted something I didn't recognize. It was wet and red and white. A strange, fat cord came out of it.

Then he turned it, and I saw it was a baby. The sound was his rough, jagged cry.

I couldn't take it. Everything in me hurt from hearing that sound. "Help him!"

Kenisha lowered the front of my gown, and the baby was placed on my chest. I pressed my hand against his back. He quieted immediately, his face against my skin.

He was upset.

And now, he was not.

Because of me.

He knew something about me that I didn't. Something that helped him.

"We have some bleeding," the doctor said. "Nurse?" Jennifer moved near him.

Kenisha pressed her hand on top of mine where it held the baby. "You did great. He's beautiful." But then a beeping made her look away. She glanced at the monitor near my head. "Doctor? Her BP?"

He focused on the space between my knees. "Did you talk to neurology?"

"Yes," Jennifer said. "They're going to do an EEG once labor is over."

"We have an abruption." His voice sounded different, harder edged. "Get that baby. Call OR to prep a room."

Kenisha covered the baby with a blanket and started to take him away. I wanted to protest, hold on to him, but my arm wouldn't do what I told it. I tried to speak, but my mouth wouldn't work.

Zigzags of light took over my vision. The room lost color.

"Doctor, she's seizing." Alarm bells sounded in the room.

I saw flowers for a moment, bending in a breeze. They were yellow, bright, and cocked to the side, as if they were turning their ears to me. They wanted to listen, to hear me speak.

I reached out for them but touched nothing.

The baby started to cry.

And then I heard nothing at all.

CHAPTER 37

Tucker

Ava had to be taken to surgery to stop her bleeding. It was a simple procedure, they'd assured me. Nothing invasive. It wouldn't slow down her recovery or keep her from having another baby. But the extra bleeding seemed to have triggered another seizure.

We were starting over again, only hours after the last time.

I waited in the labor room with Tad. He slept, rolled in a blanket, with a tiny hat on his head. Kenisha stayed with me, a hand on my shoulder. She didn't seem to hate me anymore.

The surgery didn't take long, and within a half-hour, Jennifer returned to tell us that Ava was fine and would be brought back to the room once she was out of recovery.

I hadn't told anyone Tad had been born yet. The shock of the moment when Ava seized again was still hot and sharp in my body. Then all the staff arrived. And they'd rushed her out.

I pressed my nose to Tad's cheek. Ava wouldn't even

remember she had given birth to him. She'd barely seen him before she went under.

How was I going to manage this?

I needed to tell Gram. She could be here quickly. I shifted Tad to one arm and tapped out a quick note.

Me: Tad is here. He's perfect. You can come now.

The rest of the news could wait. I skimmed everything I had missed during the emergency. Marcus was delayed. Traffic in Houston had taken an extra two hours.

Gram: On the way!

Shoot, I needed to tell her to bring the scrapbook and the laptop.

But before I could type anything else, the door opened. I thought it might be Ava returning, but a NICU nurse stepped in. "Time to take this little guy for his bath and assessment." He reached for Tad and set him into the clear plastic bed.

Kenisha stood up. "Go with the baby. This is a big photo moment, and you'll want to show them to Ava later."

I nodded and followed the clear bassinet down the hall. The three of us were buzzed into a secure area and made our way to the vast windows looking out on the hall.

They moved Tad to a bed beneath a warm lamp. He got unswaddled, which he didn't like at all. His face grew bright red as he protested the nurse washing his tiny body.

I took photos and videos. A doctor arrived and pressed a stethoscope to his chest. He moved Tad's legs and arms, testing joints. "APGAR of nine," he told the nurse. To me, he said, "He looks good and healthy."

He placed drops in Tad's eyes, then the cleaning resumed.

At one point, I looked up and noticed Gram had

arrived. She waved at us from the other side of the glass. I forced a smile. She didn't know that Ava had bled too much, seized again, and needed surgery.

I would tell her in the room.

She took pictures with her phone, tears streaking down her face. I understood. This was the first addition to our tiny family since losing my parents and brother so many years ago. She had someone new to call her own.

I pressed my finger to Tad's tiny palm, and his fingers gripped mine. He still cried, though. "I'm not Mom," I told him. "I know."

The nurse smiled up at me. She probably didn't know about Ava either, that the mother had no idea this baby existed. I pretended for a moment that I didn't know either. That we were a normal family, and this was the best day of our lives, not one full of mixed blessings and curses.

"He's a strong one," the nurse said as she slipped a onesie over Tad's head, making him cry again. I wanted to hold him close and stop his tears.

But there was so much to do with Ava. I didn't know what she would be like when she got back. We'd be starting all over for the second time in one day. The baby would be in the room. They'd expect her to feed it.

I'd have to introduce myself again. We didn't have our tools, the sequence we'd put together.

And hospitals were terrible places to figure out who you are. The smells were wrong. The food would be different. We wouldn't have a bed that seemed right or a house that felt like home.

Even so, as I looked down at Tad, I felt hope. There was an important moment when the doctor placed the baby on

Ava's chest. He stopped crying, and she seemed shocked that her body calmed him.

We read all the pregnancy books and knew that the baby would recognize Ava's heartbeat and voice. For him, she was everything. His memories of her began months ago. She wouldn't remember reading the books and learning about having a newborn, but she seemed to recognize that her baby knew her.

Hopefully, it would work again. That the wonder of a baby, and his attachment to her, would hit her at a level below memory and into her very cells.

I could handle her rejection of me. We'd been through it many times. But not Tad. She had to love him. She had to want him and be willing to care for him no matter what.

We'd been counting on it.

This would be the ultimate test of her condition.

I held his hand. He was asleep again.

The nurse gently slid the hat onto his head. "I need to make his baby burrito. Do you want to learn how?"

I stood near and watched her pull a small blanket around his body, tucking it tightly. With the hat and the burrito, only Tad's small face was visible.

"It helps them feel more secure," she said. "Wait here, and we'll get someone to escort you back to your room."

I glanced up at Gram. She wasn't taking photos anymore. She was beaming at the baby, her hands gripping the ledge below the window.

We had help. We had love.

We'd be okay.

CHAPTER 38

Ava

Bright light seared my vision, making my head pound. The only thing I knew was the *thump, thump, thump* creating pressure above my eyes.

Then I sat up, my heart racing. Where was I? What was this place?

My bed had rails. There was tape on my hand and a line running up to a bag.

The word arrived.

Hospital.

Sick people went to hospitals.

Was I sick?

I wore a strange blue dress, open in the front. I closed it over my body. My underwear was strange, stretchy mesh over paper. It didn't feel right.

I was alone. There were two doors. One was closed. The other was open. Beyond it, I spotted a sink and a mirror. *Bathroom.*

The urge to hide was strong. I swung my legs over the edge of the bed. My fuzzy socks were warm and had funny nubs on the bottom that stuck to the floor.

I only walked a few steps when a tug on my hand made me stop. The line attached to me was pulled tight. It was attached to a tall pole beside the bed. I couldn't go any farther.

I puzzled over the tube and the tape, then jerked it all off. There was a quick bite of pain, and a dot of blood welled up. I wiped it on my gown.

Voices grew louder outside the closed door. I listened, paralyzed with fear, but they kept going by. I felt exposed in the big room, so I dashed to the bathroom and closed the door behind me.

A movement almost made me scream, then I realized it was the mirror. A woman in a blue gown leaned in. We moved together. It was me.

My hair was brown, the long parts braided on both sides of my head. The skin near my eye was purple. When I touched it, pain shot through me. *Bruise.*

Something white on my wrist caught my eye. A bracelet. It had words.

Patient: Ava Giddings.

DOB: 7-7-00.

Date: 11-17-2025.

I said the name aloud. "Ava Giddings." Ava felt right. Giddings less so. I turned to the mirror. "Ava Giddings." The face there looked grim. Unhappy. I touched my cheeks. Ava Giddings.

More blood had welled up on the back of my hand. I reached for the handle of the faucet, but spotted something written on my skin. The sleeve of the gown fell back as I lifted my arm and turned my wrist.

Three lines of words, jagged and black.

Trust only this handwriting.

Find the book.

Remember your life.

Fear bolted through my body. Something inside me aligned. The terror. The urge to hide. It was real. What was my life? Why didn't I know it? Who took it?

Trust only this handwriting.

I glanced around. Mirror. Walls. White shower curtain. There were no words. Where would there be handwriting? On the bracelet? Those letters didn't match the words on my arm.

My breathing sped up so hard that I pressed my hand to my chest. I had to brave going into the big room again. Maybe the right handwriting was out there!

I listened carefully but heard nothing. I eased the door open and stepped out.

Where was the handwriting?

A whiteboard on the wall had words written on it. I approached to peer at them. At the top was "Ava Giddings." That was me. "RN Kenisha. LVN Jennifer." I had no idea who they were. The date written below the names matched my bracelet. 11-17-25.

But the handwriting wasn't the same as on my arm. It was short and angled. Mine was tall and straight.

Trust only this handwriting.

I opened the cabinets and knocked the contents onto the floor. There were cups. A pitcher. A basin. But no handwriting. The bedsheets flew through the air as I jerked them from the mattress. Nothing.

I spotted a duffel bag by the wall. Something about it felt right. I lunged for it.

Inside were clothes. Jeans. A shirt. A bra. Underwear. Shoes. Pajamas. It was stuffed tightly.

I snatched one of the shoes and shoved my foot inside. It fit.

These were my clothes. My bag.

The gown hit the floor, and I stripped off the weird paper underwear. The inside was red with blood.

I paused. A hospital was for sick people.

But then I saw something else. More words on my skin.

Ava Roberts. 7-7-00.

Those were written in *the same handwriting* as on my arm.

But wait. I checked my bracelet again.

Patient: Ava Giddings.

The names didn't match. Something was wrong.

I read the words on my other hip.

Mom is bad.

Panic flashed over me, hot and furious. I had to get away. Now. Mother could be anywhere.

I jerked the shirt over my head, dragged on the underwear, and pulled on the jeans. Those were wildly loose, so I stuffed the bottom of my shirt in the waist to keep them from falling down.

When my shoes were on, I lifted the bag.

Below it was a big book.

When I read the front of it, sparks flew behind my eyes.

Trust only this handwriting.

This is the book.

Remember your life.

I compared to my arm.

This was it!

I flipped open to a random page and read a few lines.

Do not trust Mother.

   I have to run away.

· · ·

The book was telling me to run away!

I had to go. Now.

I shoved the book into the bag and put it on my shoulder.

Where was I going?

It didn't matter. I had to *go*.

I eased the door open. A few people walked by. I waited. I realized my name was on the board. I rushed over and smeared it with my fist so the letters couldn't be read. Mother could never know I was here.

I checked the hall. There was only one woman, and she was walking away.

I squeezed out the door and hurried away to find some place safe to read the rest of my book.

CHAPTER 39
Tucker

Baby Tad's assessment was finally done. He'd stopped crying, totally spent from the effort of protesting his new predicament.

"Baby looks good." The nurse patted Tad's belly. "I'll walk with you back to the room. You want to push?"

I nodded. I gripped the handle at the end of the clear bassinet, and we headed to the secure doors. I steeled myself for what I'd find when I got to our room. Would Ava be back? Awake? Would they have to strap her down again? Would she be screaming?

Maybe I shouldn't take the baby.

"This way," the nurse said, pointing to the right. "We have to navigate the maze."

Gram met us in the hall. "What is the status of everything?" she asked.

Time to break the news. "She had blood loss from labor. They had to do a minor surgery. They think the blood loss caused another seizure right after he was born."

Gram's blue-veined hand lifted to her mouth. "Tucker. Oh, no. Is she all right?"

"They said the surgery was simple. I don't know if she's back in the room yet or not."

Gram tucked her phone away. The happy enthusiasm was gone. "I went to the room before the nurse told me to go to the nursery to find you. I left the duffle bag and the scrapbook there."

"You brought the memory book?"

"Yes. I found it in her office. And her phone on the floor in the kitchen."

Relief crashed over me. "Good. I forgot to tell you to get them. She might not even know she gave birth. We've never been through two restarts back to back."

Our grim gazes locked. I knew what she was thinking, how hard all the resets had been. And this time, we'd have Tad.

My mind raced as we followed the nurse down the hall. Ava would be in no shape to take care of him alone for quite some time.

"You'll start working with her right away, won't you?" Gram's voice was high with tension. She knew.

"I will. Ava made that book as airtight as possible. The mystery of her mother helps the most. She's motivated to read and learn once she connects the book to her tattoos."

Gram patted my arm. "It will be all right. Have faith."

We passed the nurse's station that I remembered from our arrival. We were nearly there.

I glanced at all the doors with their blue and pink ribbons. I should get one for Tad.

A door halfway down the hall stood open. Was that ours?

I hoped not.

I wanted to speed up, but I was pushing the baby. Tad

was sleeping peacefully in his blanket burrito. I drew in a breath to fight the urge to run.

Gram noticed. "What's wrong?"

My throat constricted. "I think our door is open." I stopped the bassinet, and the nurse looked back at us.

"Wait here with the baby," I said, choking on the words.

I closed the distance to the door in a mad dash.

Please be sleeping. Please let it be a nurse who left it open. Maybe the neurologist is in there.

I pushed it wide.

The bed was empty, the sheets stripped and on the floor. The blue gown sat beside them, along with the postpartum underwear. I raced into the bathroom and threw aside the white curtain.

She had been here. And now, she was gone.

When I returned to the main room, Gram had arrived. The nurse and Tad were in the hall.

"Where is she?" Gram asked.

My gut tightened. "I don't know." The cabinet was open. Cups and a pitcher lay on the floor.

Gram's shaky finger pointed to the whiteboard.

Ava's name had been hastily wiped through.

Gram sank onto the bed. "That poor girl."

"Stay with the baby. I'm going to get security. Maybe she's wandering around."

The confused nurse pushed the bassinet inside. "Is everything all right?" Her eyes grew wide as she took in the room.

I didn't have time to explain things to her. I needed to find Kenisha or Jennifer. They knew what she looked like and what had happened. Hopefully, they could help me find Ava before she got too far.

I paused for a moment, glancing around. "Where did you leave our bag?"

Gram gestured toward the corner. "Over there. The bag was on top of the scrapbook. They're both gone."

I stared at the empty corner. She must have tried on her clothes and figured out they were hers. Then, she left with everything. A terrifying mystery to solve. A dead panic.

Our new family was already in peril.

CHAPTER 40

Ava

The halls went on and on. There were so many people. Anyone could be looking for me. Anyone could be Mom.

I kept my head down and didn't meet anyone's gaze. Finally, I reached a big open section with a glass rail. Far below was the ground, with more people walking around.

Something dinged behind me. Wide doors opened. People went in and out. Arrows pointed up and down. My brain whirred. Then the word arrived. *Elevator.*

I raced inside as it closed. The doors bumped my bag and opened again.

Come on. Close. Close. Close!

Three other people were inside. One held a big vase full of red flowers. The other two stood close together. They paid no attention to me. I was still safe.

The elevator went down, down. My stomach felt strange, like it was lifting inside my body.

Then the doors opened to noise and a different type of air.

Here, people walked in every direction. There were so

many smells. I didn't know what any of them were, but they made my stomach rumble.

I walked swiftly to the middle of the space. I looked up and could see all the floors, including the one where I came from. I dashed away. I couldn't have anyone see me from up there! Someone there knew my name. They had written it on the board for anyone to find, including Mom.

Mom was bad.

The sun blasted through enormous windows, a whole wall of them. I headed that way. People walked through doors that slid open by themselves. I rushed toward them and burst out to the other side.

The sky opened wide. It was pleasantly warm outdoors. I clutched my bag and walked along the sidewalk. There were cars everywhere, rows and rows of them. Did I have one here somewhere? I sensed I could open a door and sit behind one of the wheels. But I couldn't picture what to do. And I had no way of knowing which one might be mine.

I walked for a while, the big hospital building far behind me, when my body started to hurt in several places. The back of my hand where the blood came out. The purple bruise near my eye.

And between my legs. Down there, it hurt more and more until I couldn't walk anymore. It hurt too much.

A bench ahead had a lone man sitting on it. I collapsed onto the other end, pressing the bag tight to my belly. The pain eased some but throbbed in a steady rhythm.

A hospital was for sick people.

Maybe I shouldn't have left. I could see the big building in the distance. I could go back.

Trust only this handwriting.

The man on the bench stared at me, his jaw working

back and forth like he was going to talk. His beard was thick and wild, and his pants were torn at the knees. He leaned toward me. My fear of what he might do or say, that he might know my mother or tell her where I was, became bigger than my pain.

I launched away and walked a little farther until the pain got too bad again. I reached an empty bench and almost stumbled trying to sit down. Something was making me weak. I couldn't keep going.

I stretched out to cover the entire bench, so no one could sit next to me. I rested my head on the bag and watched people walk by and cars move along the street. No one looked at me for long, their gaze darting away when they spotted me. The sun shone down, so I closed my eyes.

I lay there until finally, the pain lessened. I no longer felt like I would collapse.

I sat up and unzipped the bag. Something jingled. I dug along the side and pulled it out.

Keys.

But for what?

One of them read "Ford." Another had only letters and numbers. A disk held them together, worn and rough around the edge. It was bright blue with a coffee mug on one side. I flipped it over.

Big Harry's Diner. Good eats. 430 First Street.

Is this where the key fit?

I peered out beyond the sidewalk. What street was this? How could I tell?

Cars passed, the sun blasting off the shiny paint. The pain started to rise again, throbbing like a heartbeat.

Maybe I should go back to the hospital.

I went through more of the bag and pulled out a green

bottle. The words were strange, sideways, but I could read them. *Mountain Dew.* I untwisted the top, and pale liquid spewed everywhere. I held the bottle over the sidewalk until it stopped.

My hand was sticky and wet. I licked it, and the taste was so good, so perfect, that I quickly brought the bottle to my lips.

The liquid was sweet and warm and made my stomach stop rumbling. I drank half of the bottle before I stopped for a breath.

So much better. I was still in pain, but I felt like I could go on.

I twisted the cap back in place and wiped my hands on my jeans. There was more to look at, including the important notebook.

I glanced around. A woman watched me closely, then turned her gaze to my book.

I covered it with a shirt from the bag. I couldn't read it out here. It wasn't safe.

I was about to zip the bag again when I spotted a small bottle. I stared at the label. "Ibuprofen tablets. 200 mg. For pain relief."

Pain relief. I needed that.

I read the label out loud. "Take one pill every four to six hours. Two pills may be taken."

I tried to open the top. It wouldn't twist like the Mountain Dew did. I banged it on the bench, but that didn't help. It was too tough. I wanted to cry. I needed pain relief.

I set the bottle down. *Breathe. Breathe. Breathe.*

Car after car after car drove by. Another woman approached. She was talking to herself. I listened to what she was saying.

"Lila, we can't accept that offer. It will put us upside down." She huffed. "I won't do it!"

Her tone made me shrink back against the back of the bench. Not her. I couldn't ask her.

No one else was anywhere on the sidewalk.

My eyes pricked like they'd been hurt. I brushed my hands against them. Tears. I didn't know crying could hurt.

I simply had to open the bottle. I had too many things that hurt.

I examined the lid. There were arrows and an image of a hand. I couldn't understand what to do. I squeezed my eyes closed, so frustrated, then unexpectedly, my hands pushed down and turned, and the lid fell away.

They knew what to do. I just had to stop trying.

What else did my body know that I didn't?

I shook two pills onto my lap. They were small and orange.

I put them in my mouth, rolling them around with my tongue. My teeth scraped against them, filling my mouth with a horrible taste.

I spat them into my palm, breathing hard again. Why was everything so difficult?

I opened the Mountain Dew and took another drink.

But the moment I lowered the bottle, my other hand popped the pills in my mouth. They went down with the rest of the drink.

I had swallowed them whole.

Magic.

I was magic.

I drank the Mountain Dew until it was gone and placed the empty bottle back in the bag. I managed to close the pill bottle and tucked it in next to it.

I glanced around. No one was coming. I could risk looking at the book.

I opened it in the middle. The pages had photographs. One of them was me, but I looked different. My hair was down, not in two braids. But it was definitely me. My nose. My eyes. I was surrounded by pots of flowers, most of them yellow. The blooms looked like stars with a funny round snout.

Standing next to me and the pots was a woman with a wrap on her head. Her skin was dark, while I was pale. She smiled, while I was serious. She was tall and substantial. I was small, like I was disappearing into the pots. Beneath it were written the words "Ava and Maya."

The next one showed me with a man. He had straight, short hair and blue eyes. Our heads touched together as we smiled. This one said, "Ava and Tucker."

A brother? A boyfriend?

Why didn't I know?

I turned the page. This photo showed me with another man, gray tinting parts of his hair. This one said, "Ava and her father Marcus."

I had a father!

Where was he?

Why didn't he save me from Mother?

I pressed my hand to my thigh where I had seen the tattoo.

Mom is bad.

I glanced to make sure no one was coming and went back to the first page.

Mother stole the last book.

I can't believe it.

How could she!
I knew things were missing. I knew it!
I hate her! I hate her! I hate her!

My breath came in pants, and I pressed my hand to my mouth.

I knew it.

Something felt wrong.

I wouldn't have these words on my skin if something wasn't wrong.

Another woman drew near to my bench, and I pulled the notebook to my chest to hide the words. Could she be my mother?

The woman kept walking, but the fear remained. Anyone could see me here.

I glanced over at the hospital. Did my mother put me there? Was that why I woke up so afraid? Was she why I hurt? Why I had a bruise on my face?

There was blood in my underwear.

Panic welled up. What did she do?

The building was too close. I had to get far away.

I stood up. I felt stronger. My stomach didn't rumble. The Mountain Dew took that away. The pain was less. The pills might be working.

I shoved the notebook into my bag. I walked another block, careful to take it slow. But I felt better as more time passed. The ache between my legs lessened.

The cars got fewer as I moved away from the hospital. Soon, there were houses along the street. Then, a block full of tall grass and trees.

I darted into the trees and walked away from the road.

I was safe here, hidden among the brush. I couldn't see the hospital or even the street anymore.

I found a bare spot on the ground and unpacked the bag completely. There were more clothes. A shirt with the words "Austin Community College" across the top. Another clue, maybe. A pair of shorts. More underwear. Socks. Then something curious. A small blanket. It was pale blue with dinosaurs. The urge was strong to lift it to my face.

It smelled clean and fresh. My chest loosened. This was a good thing, something happy. I set it in my lap.

I removed the empty Mountain Dew. The keys. The notebook. I found two more small bags. One had a comb, a lip balm, a tube of toothpaste, and two toothbrushes.

Why two?

The other bag held several chocolate bars. I read the wrappers. Hershey's. Twix. Mr. Goodbar. I tore one open. It had gone soft, but I gobbled it down. It tasted so good. I closed my eyes for a moment. I was okay. I got away. I had a book to help me. I got rid of my pain. And I ate something.

I was going to be all right.

I opened the notebook again.

So much has happened since that first entry in the notebook. So much. I kept it there to remind you to be careful. It always gets your attention, and the handwriting matches your tattoo. But there is a lot to know, Ava. Take your time.

I've organized and reorganized this information to help you reorient yourself to your life when you lose your memory. You can trust it.

There are people you need to know. Safe people.

Tucker. Dad. Gram. Maya. Big Harry.

I've tried over and over to put our life story into a form that will work. Sometimes you—or, me, I guess—are mean or scared when we come back after losing our memories. You don't want to listen to anyone. You resist being helped.

I'm still trying to find a way to keep us safe when this happens.

But please read this. All of it. I learned not to put in addresses or phone numbers because things change. Life changes. One time you went to the most dangerous place of all by accident because of a location you found in this notebook.

I hope I've fixed it now.

Read, Ava. Sit and learn. Trust no one who talks to you, approaches you, or takes you anywhere until you have all the answers.

Find a safe place. Be careful of police or hospitals. Sometimes they send you where you should not go because that is what they have on record.

Learn everything first. You are here, inside these pages. But you are also inside yourself. Your brain has disconnected your memories, but we don't only remember with our minds. We remember with smells, with tastes, with feelings. With muscles that automatically do things we didn't know we could do.

I looked at my hands. It was true. They had opened the pill bottle.

You can take photographs, Ava. You studied it in college. You can drive a car. You can do math in your head and flip an omelet even if you're half asleep.

And you can love, even when you're sure you can't. When Tucker finds you, try not to be scared. One thing we've figured out over all these memory resets is that love and fear are divided by a painfully narrow line. Don't resist Tucker. He is the one who has always kept you safe.

It's time to read about who you are. I'm sorry there are so few entries from when we were young. Mother destroyed almost all of those. Some of this story you wrote yourself. Other parts were done by Tucker.

Keep this story, Ava. Protect it at all cost. It's why words are tattooed on your body.

Trust only this handwriting.

This is the book.

Remember your life.

CHAPTER 41
Tucker

Nurse Kenisha alerted the hospital security about Ava. Everyone started looking for her. All exits were watched.

But at this point, I'd been sitting on Ava's bed for over an hour, holding baby Tad, absolutely terrified. Too much time was passing. I didn't think she was hiding in a mop closet. She left. I knew it.

Nurse Kenisha was pissed as hell. Nurse Jennifer was supposed to stay with Ava in recovery, but she'd gotten paged to another room. Kenisha was supposed to be off shift, but she refused to leave, going through the hospital herself. Only a few people knew what Ava looked like. Even fewer knew about her condition.

Gram rubbed my back. "We'll find her, Tucker. We always do."

"We lost her for half a year in 2018."

She sighed. "I know."

Tad woke with a startled cry. I moved him to my shoulder, but he didn't like that position. His face turned beet red.

"Let me take him," Gram said. "You page the nurse for some formula."

I pushed the red button on the bed. We were allowed to stay in the room until Tad was discharged, which would be tomorrow if Ava didn't return. I couldn't possibly leave. Ava had a hospital wristband. She might come back here.

I pressed the heel of my hand to my eye. No, she specifically warned herself about police and hospitals, literally on page two of her book. We did that to prevent another situation like in 2019 when a police report showed her last known location as her mother's house.

The notebook would have no addresses or phone numbers. We took them out. And she wouldn't remember having a baby, anyway. There was no reason for her to come back. Whatever made her run, made her search the room and erase her name, might scare her even after reading the notebook.

It felt hopeless.

Gram had the touch because Tad got quiet in her arms. "Let's go over it again. What is in the bag?"

"Extra clothes. Some treats we planned to sneak in—a drink, chocolate. Some ibuprofen. Toiletries."

"Does the notebook talk about her father?"

"Yes, she'll know they found each other."

"Can she go to him?"

"Not with the information in it. There are no addresses."

As if Marcus could sense we were talking about him, he buzzed my phone. He had to be nearly here. The last time he checked in, I told him Tad had arrived, and Ava was in surgery. Things happened so fast after that, and I hadn't thought to update him.

He was going to be so upset. My stomach clenched as I unlocked my phone.

Marcus: How is Ava?

Gram glanced at the screen. "What are you going to tell him?"

"I don't know."

"Just give it to him straight. It's not the first time you've had to find her together."

She was right.

Me: Ava is missing.

I could practically feel Marcus hitting the brakes. I wondered if he would pull over to text or just call.

But he must have been at a stoplight because he texted again.

Marcus: How long ago?

Me: About an hour now. I was in the nursery with Tad.

Marcus: What set her off?

Me: She woke up alone. Took the bag and notebook.

Marcus: Can she make it home with that?

Me: No. We removed all addresses from it.

Marcus: I'm in the city. Be there in half an hour.

I dropped the phone onto the bed.

"Anything else in the bag?" Gram asked.

"I think she put her keys in it. I'm pretty sure."

"Could she find her way home with them?"

"No. But there's a keychain for Big Harry's Diner. It has an address."

Gram stood up, patting the baby's back. "Call over there. Now. She might have made her way to the restaurant."

I couldn't see how. The restaurant was a good ten miles from the hospital. And Ava just had a baby. She had to be in pain walking. She wouldn't have any money for a bus or her phone to call a ride.

But Gram was still right. I should give Harry the heads-up. He was one of the few people Ava trusted no matter how she came out of a reset.

"Where else could she possibly go?" Gram asked. "We have to assume she'll find addresses on her own. She might find a police officer or one might find her. They could look her up by her name. She probably found the name and birth date tattoo when she got dressed. The system will have records from when she ran away from her mother, plus the restraining order."

Gram was thinking straighter than I was.

"Her name and birthdate were on the hospital wristband, too. If the police pick her up, they might know about the shelter and her mother's house."

Gram paced with Tad. "Call that lady at the shelter who remembers Ava."

"Sheila."

"Yes. Sheila. Do they have a book?"

"Yes, but it's old."

"What's in it?"

"Maya's duplex. Big Harry's. Her old apartment. Maybe your house."

"Will Sheila call you if she shows up there?"

"Maybe. But only if it's actually Sheila she finds. Otherwise, no, if she shows up with the police, they won't tell anyone she's there. That's why it's a shelter."

Gram stared out the window, shifting from side to side, holding Tad tightly to her chest. "Should someone be driving around here?"

Nurse Kenisha walked in right as Gram asked the question. "I'll do that. The police aren't terribly helpful since she's an adult. They practically need a court order stating she didn't abandon her motherly duties."

"How about hospital security?" I asked.

"They're walking the perimeter. There's not a soul on shift who doesn't know about Ava."

"Thank you," Gram said. "And thank you for driving."

Kenisha tugged on her lanyard. "I feel responsible. She shouldn't have been left alone."

She got that right.

"Who else can drive around the neighborhood?" Gram asked.

"I can call Bill. He'll do it," I said.

"Before I start driving, what do you need for this little guy?" Kenisha asked.

"We already paged our regular nurse," I said. "I guess start him on formula since Ava's gone."

"I'll get her in here." Kenisha headed for the door. "My number is on the board. Let me know if Ava turns up."

I sat on the sofa by the window to alert Big Harry, Maya, and Sheila and to ask Bill to help. "Do you think the police could find her current address?" I asked Gram.

"Maybe. Let Isadora know."

I texted as fast as I could. A new nurse arrived. This one was young and friendly, all blonde ponytail and happy smile. "What does that baby boy need?" She clearly didn't know anything yet.

When everyone was texted, I stared out the window. It would be dark soon. There was a mile of parking lots, a big busy street, and then a residential area beyond the commercial blocks. Ava could be anywhere.

It didn't matter that the police weren't helping yet. Ava was wily and would be warned about them from the notebook. We'd been through this before. The only way they would be involved is if she collapsed somewhere and someone called them on her behalf.

God. Had that happened? Maybe we should call the other hospitals.

So much to do. So much.

Tad had quieted again. Gram had moved to the rocking chair in the corner, the baby in her arms.

He needed his mother.

We all did.

CHAPTER 42

Ava

I looked up into the trees. Birds flitted around, chasing each other. A breeze ruffled the leaves. Despite learning what was wrong with me, that I'd lost my memory, I felt content and calm.

I had done the right thing. Ava said to avoid police and hospitals. I was glad I had left. She was right. I listened to myself and got away.

I'd already learned so much.

I was a photographer.

I could make an omelet.

I had someone who loved me and kept me safe. Tucker. Where was he now? Where was my mother? How did she fit in? I ran my hands over the words on my arm. It was a tattoo. The warning was so important that I put it on my skin forever.

I could trust Maya, whoever she was. Wait, was she the one in the photograph? I flipped until I found it again, looking at myself, the woman, and the pots of flowers. It made sense that I would give myself photos of the good people.

And I could trust Big Harry. I pulled out the keychain. Another clue. It was coming together.

Old Ava told me to read. She warned me to pay attention.

I would try.

I paged through the book, my eyes pausing on random words.

Disco room.

Seizures.

Tucker.

Mother.

Fear.

Run away.

Home.

Shelter.

Big Harry.

There was so much here. I didn't know how long it would take me to read. I skipped to the end, hoping there were instructions. Couldn't I just go to the part where it told me what to do?

But the last page only said, "Time to watch the video."

What video?

I pulled another one of the candy bars from the bag and unwrapped it, looking around before I started reading again. A woman walked a small dog through the grass. Her dog spotted me and trotted over until it reached the end of its leash.

I held my breath, but no panic came. I wasn't afraid of dogs. And I sensed that someone with a dog would be safe.

The woman gave a small wave. I waved back. The dog ran in another direction to pee on a tree. This made me smile.

This was a good place. Old Ava would approve.

I flipped back to the beginning of the notebook and moved to the third page. Maybe somewhere it would tell me where to go to find Tucker or Maya or Harry.

This page had a drawing, crudely made. A man figure. A woman. And a child. There were trees and flowers, and the three figures held hands. Beneath were the words, "Mom. Ava. Dad." There was a stamp in the corner, a circle with the words, "Good work!"

At the bottom, there was handwriting I recognized. It read, "2006. Age 6. It looks like you used to go to regular school. This is your only image of your father. There are no photos of him in the house. Mother didn't allow it."

No photos of my father when I was six? I had them now. Why wouldn't Mother allow it?

I flipped the page to find out.

2006 - Age 16

I've been so lost. Time has disuppeared.

Grandma Flowers has been watching me. I like to sit on her porch. I'm not allowed to go inside her half of the duplex. Mother says so. Only the porch.

Grandma Flowers told me she had some books I liked to read before I forgot everything. She got my favorite one so I could read it again.

But something strange happened.

I opened the cover, and there were three lines. They said.

Trust only this handwriting.

Find the book.

Remember your life.

Grandma Flowers and I looked at each other.

Her face pinched, and her mouth tightened. "Something's not right."

I flipped through the book and found words that were highlighted. The first was the word "available," but only the AVA part was highlighted.

So, it was a note for me. I picked out each word and wrote it down.

Mother has hidden your life. Find the notes. They are everywhere. Get out. She is doing something to make you forget. Run. Go. Escape.

My heart hammered, and it was hard to breathe. I didn't know what to do.

I asked her for any other books I read before I lost time. Grandma Flowers brought me a big stack. They all had highlighted parts. Some of them told me the locations of the notes I had hidden. I have paper flowers all over the wall of my bedroom, and each one hides a tiny note on the back side.

One told me to write on my belly the same words I saw inside the novel.

Trust only this handwriting.

Find the book.

Remember your life

Another told me I have a real dad.

Lots of them said not to trust Mother.

I have to run away.

2007 - Age 17

I'm going to the hospital.

. . .

My head snapped up. The hospital! I looked back the way I'd come, but I couldn't see the building anymore. Maybe this would tell me what I needed to know! I clutched the book and continued reading.

Grandma Flowers asked a lot of questions, and now, Mother doesn't let me see her.

Mother says in the hospital they will make a seizure happen on purpose, so they can study my brain and figure out how to help me.

I know I will lose my memory again. And Mother will be in the room.

I'll have to hide the notes I've put together. But I'll need them. No telling what she could do there. I don't know what her plan is. She says it's to help me, but my gut says no.

I'm scared.

I'm going to take my biggest textbook History of the World *and tape these notes inside. I'll have to break all my rules. Removing pages from my notebook. Carrying them with me. Rules that have kept me sane and let me know the things Mother wants to hide.*

I won't take everything. I'm not crazy. I'm making double and triple copies of things, writing it all out again and again, especially the warning.

I'll make it through somehow.

Wish me luck.

The trees rustled, and I realized it was getting dark. The

white page glowed in the dying light but was getting hard to read.

Alarm filled me. I couldn't stay here. I needed light.

I peered through the trees. There was a glow near the street. And benches. I itched my legs. That would be better than the ground.

I gathered my things. Toothbrush bag. Chocolate bar. Empty Mountain Dew. Pill bottle. Notebook. Keys. Clothes.

The blanket was still on my lap. I lifted it to my nose again. I compared the smell to the other clothes. It was different. The clothes seem familiar. But the blanket didn't. Why was that?

I had no idea. I put it all away and zipped the bag.

The light fell so fast by the time I started walking that I kept losing my footing on the rough terrain. But I aimed for the light and finally broke through the trees to the road.

I could sit on the sidewalk and read, but it felt so open, so dangerous. I wished I had a hood to pull up like some of the people who had walked by me earlier.

Instead, I kept my head down as I decided which way to go. Back toward the hospital or to someplace new?

The decision was easy. There was a covered bench ahead. It had a top and sides, creating a small shelter. I headed for it, planning to scrunch into the corner while I read. But when I reached it, another man was already there, drinking from a bottle wrapped in a paper bag.

I halted. Should I keep going? This place was so good.

The man spoke in a low, rumbling voice. "Nice night we're having."

He was the first person who'd ever talked directly to me. I didn't know what to say back. Was this a nice night? It was dark and colder than the day.

He didn't seem to mind that I hadn't answered him. "The bus will be here in fifteen minutes."

A bus. I could get around town on a bus. Get far away fast.

I smashed myself into the opposite corner of the bench and set my bag on my lap. I pulled the notebook out.

"You like to read?" he asked.

I opened my mouth. Instead of words, I coughed. My throat felt raw. Eventually, I managed to say, "Yes." The sound was strange to my ears.

I hoped that by answering his question, I could get to the rest of the story, but he kept going. "My mama used to read to me. Did yours?"

I had no idea, but based on what I knew of her, I said, "I don't think so."

He grunted and took another swig. He seemed to be done talking, so I returned to my story. I needed to finish. Then I would know everything, and I could decide what to do.

CHAPTER 43
Tucker

As night fell, despair blanketed the room.

Gram continued rocking Tad, who had taken his first bottle. Or an ounce of one, anyway.

Marcus called everyone under the sun, pacing with his ear to the phone. The shelter. The police. Hospital staff. The volunteer agency that walked parts of Austin to help the unhoused, the hungry, the lost.

The only thing he hadn't made headway with was getting the hospital to turn over the security footage. There were procedures for that due to HIPPA laws, and the offices had already closed.

But he had a lawyer ready to go after them the moment the administrative offices reopened.

He glanced over at me. "We should have had twenty-four-hour care for her the minute she got pregnant. Someone who stayed with her no matter what."

Ava wouldn't have wanted that. But I understood his frustration. His fear. Ava was out there, post-partum, post-surgery, alone, no money, no help. She could be kidnapped, trafficked, abused.

I stood up abruptly. I couldn't think like that. Ava was smart. And suspicious. She had most likely holed up somewhere until she figured something out.

Tina had made it into town and offered to stay at Gram's in case Ava showed up there. Maya was waiting at the duplex. Harry was standing guard at Ava's old apartment, and his staff was watching for her at his diner.

The hospital was shutting down, and only the emergency room entrance would be accessible soon. But the security guards knew to watch for a confused woman who might come up to any door. We had to trust they would notice her.

Sheila didn't work at the shelter anymore, but Beatrice, who served as the director now, said she'd be watching for anyone with Ava's description.

Bill and Kenisha had put posters on all the telephone polls in the area and signs in the business windows. Marcus had convinced the police to put out an APB on her, even though normally you had to wait twenty-four hours. He was good like that. He knew the right people to call to get things done.

He spoke into his phone after a long pause. "Be ready to go before a judge the moment the courts open. I'm going to push this. I want to see the moment she left her room on that footage." Then he shoved his phone in his pocket and stared out at the night.

The room got quiet, so we all startled when he said, "We have to call her."

We all knew who he meant.

Gram shook her head. "Ava didn't want her mother here."

"It's where she ended up last time," Marcus said.

He was right. And Geneva had surely figured out Ava

was pregnant. She stalked her everywhere and knew at least roughly where we lived.

Marcus spoke again. "You want me to do it?"

I stood up. "No, I will."

Marcus was too antagonistic in moments like these. I lifted my phone from the side table and unplugged the charging cord. If Geneva had gotten to Ava, we needed to handle her carefully.

Could she have known Ava had come here in labor? Had a seizure? Had she known she would be vulnerable and led her right out the door?

We couldn't ignore the possibility.

I clicked on her contact name and let out a long breath. I had to do this exactly right.

Geneva answered in a suspiciously antagonistic tone. "What can I do for you, Tucker?"

The moment I heard her voice, I shifted tactics. "We wanted to update you on Ava."

She immediately changed. "Is she all right? Did she have another seizure? Oh, my God. Where are you?"

She was too frantic. She didn't have her. But just in case, I said, "Are you aware of her situation lately?"

Her voice rose another notch. "What do you mean? Are the seizures worse? Is she getting brain damage?"

Marcus watched me intently. Maybe I should let him hear this, too. I switched to speaker.

"She doesn't have brain damage, and her seizures are about the same," I said.

There was a pause, then Geneva spoke again, her voice breaking. "I wish you all would listen to me. My treatment works the best."

I glanced at Marcus. He nodded at me to continue.

"I understand your position," I said. "We all want Ava to be better."

"So, what is the update on her? You scared me half to death!"

I lifted my eyebrows at Marcus.

His lips pursed. Then he said, "Geneva, she has gone missing again."

I was glad he was the one to say it. I wondered if he would mention the baby. Or if we should.

"Again?" Geneva laughed. "And you think I magically stole her. You two couldn't keep a homing pigeon in the right place."

Marcus tightened his hands into fists. "We wanted to update you on this so you could keep watch. We'd appreciate it if you let us know if she turns up near you."

Geneva laughed again. "Right, so you can keep me away from her all over again. Fat chance. I'll start looking, though." She hung up.

I shoved my phone into my pocket. "That went well."

Marcus rubbed his chin. "You know, I don't think she's aware Ava was pregnant."

"She didn't ask about the baby," I said.

Gram spoke up from the corner. "Or else she didn't want you two to know she knew."

"Well, she's looking for her now," Marcus said. "I'll put a tail on her. She won't take off with her again." He started tapping on his phone.

We had no more aces to play.

But for all we knew, Ava had found someone who could look her up online. If she had done that, the road might lead straight back to her mother.

CHAPTER 44

Ava

The book was done. I got back to the final page that read, "Time to watch the video."

I closed it.

The man on the bench glanced over. "Was it good?"

I couldn't answer. I wasn't sure how to feel.

"Not good, then?"

He lifted his bottle to his mouth, realized it was empty, and flung it toward the trash can. It tipped over the edge and fell in with a clank. He arranged a dirty, torn brown blanket over his knees.

The night was getting chillier. There wasn't anything like the man was wearing in the bag, a jacket with sleeves and a zipper in front. I could probably put on more than one shirt, though. I shifted the bag to find one.

"You got a problem, girlie," the man said, waving his hand toward my chest.

I looked down. Two big wet circles had formed on my shirt.

I pulled the fabric away from my skin. What was that? The wetness was making me even colder.

"You got a baby, then, I reckon?" he asked.

What did he mean? My breathing sped up, like I was out of air. What was happening to me? I huffed harder and faster.

"You okay, girlie? Did your baby die or something?"

I flung the book back open. Among all the pictures was another one of me and Tucker, the very last one. I was big in that picture, my belly all swollen.

I wasn't that big now.

I read the words below it. I'd skipped them because I knew the picture was me and Tucker.

Our last photo before the baby comes.

I let out a cry.

A baby! The blanket in my bag!

I pulled it out. It was small because it was for a *baby*.

It smelled different from my clothes because it was for a *baby*.

I was in the hospital because I'd had a *baby*.

I hurt between my legs because I'd had a *baby*.

My heart pounded. I had to go. I had to find the baby. I pressed my hand to my belly. It was soft and squishy, like something was missing from inside.

Did my baby die?

Or did I run from it?

I shoved the notebook in the bag but didn't waste time zipping it up. I ran down the long sidewalk.

My feet hurt, and the pain came back, worse than before. My chest joined in, cold and clammy and aching as I moved.

A baby. A baby. A baby.

Eventually, the bright building became visible. As I dashed toward it, I spotted something that set off alarm bells in my head. I ignored it, but it kept happening, again and again.

I finally stopped to look.

It was me. My picture. It was on every pole, every metal box. I turned in a circle. On windows. Walls. Me, my picture, my name.

I reached for one and pulled it down.

Ava Roberts. Ava Giddings. Missing. Please call this number to contact husband Tucker Giddings or father Marcus Roberts.

Some photos were of me and the man from my bag. The one where our foreheads touch. The others were me with the gray-haired man. Some were just me. Smiling. Serious.

But they all said the same thing.

Ava Roberts. Ava Giddings. Missing.

Both of those names were me. I was Ava Roberts because my father was Marcus Roberts. I became Ava Giddings to match Tucker Giddings. I married the man from the notebook. We had a baby.

I clutched the paper as I ran hard. The pain was terrible, but I kept going.

I approached the big sliding door where I'd left.

It didn't open.

I pressed my hands to the glass. A sign read, "Enter through Emergency."

What did that mean? How could I enter through an emergency?

The pain was incredible. I clutched my bag to my belly, crumpling the paper. I needed inside. The lights were on. Why had they closed the doors?

Then I heard a voice. "Ava? Ava Giddings?"

I turned. A man in dark blue shone a flashlight my way.

"Yes," I said. "I'm Ava Giddings."

He stood halfway out of an open door farther down. He looked inside the building. "I've got her!"

I tried to step toward him, but everything hurt too much. I leaned against the wall, hanging on to the bag.

"Bring a wheelchair!" the man called. "Hold on, Ava. We'll get you some help." He rushed toward me and placed an arm around my waist to hold me up. "Are you okay?"

My vision wavered from the pain, but I said, "Where is Tucker? Where is the baby?"

"Your family is here. They're in your room."

"They're here?"

"Yes. We've been looking for you all day."

Soon, I was surrounded by people. A woman in pink rolled out a wheelchair. The first man helped me into it, setting the bag in my lap.

Two more people in uniform came over. We squeezed through the small door to the elevator I took when I ran.

I was going back!

Lots of people in colored clothes looked at me as I passed them in the halls. They smiled and brushed their hands against my shoulder.

I wanted to go faster and, despite the pain, almost jumped out of the wheelchair to run again. But then we turned down a hall, and I saw the people from the picture.

The man who leaned his head against mine. Tucker Giddings.

The one with the graying hair. My father. Marcus Roberts.

Then a small woman with gray curls. Gram.

She held a bundle in her arms.

I didn't care about the pain anymore. I tossed the bag to the side and launched from the wheelchair.

"Whoa, Ava!" someone behind me said, but I ignored them. I ran again, energy sparking through me.

When I reached them, I stopped. I didn't look at the other people. They didn't matter.

Only this one did.

He was wrapped in a white blanket with pink and blue stripes. His tiny face showed beneath a stretchy hat.

He opened his eyes. I knew those eyes. My whole body pricked with recognition. As he watched me, his mouth opened in a long, easy yawn.

I smiled, my body calming, the alarm bells no longer ringing in my ears. This was where I was supposed to be.

"Back down you go," someone said, and I was pressed back into the wheelchair.

Tucker bent down. "You want to hold him?"

I nodded, still looking into the tiny eyes.

Then he was in my arms. I tingled everywhere. My belly. My chest. My shirt got more wet.

I knew him. I knew him with every part of my body.

They wheeled me into the room I'd run from, but I could only stare at his blue eyes. My eyes. We were the same.

Everyone seemed to be crying. My father. My husband. Gram. But not me.

And not this baby.

We could only look at each other.

There was no way I would ever not know that he was mine.

Epilogue: Ava

The screen in front of me went black for a moment. I started to get up, thinking the video was done, but Rosie whined and put her paw on my leg.

"I can't go yet?" I asked her.

Rosie left her paw in place.

I settled back down. "Well, all right."

The blackness blinked into color and sound. Okay, yes. There was another one.

It was me again, this time with longer hair. I lifted my hand to my shorter style. I wasn't sure which one was better.

In the video, I sat on a blue sofa and held out my arms.

A small boy toddled slowly and carefully toward me. He wore blue overalls, and his feet were bare.

In the video, my eyes lit up. "Come on, Tad! Come on! You're doing it!"

The words were barely out when Tad abruptly sat on his bottom. His face screwed up in a terrible pout, then he let out a wail.

I scooped him onto my lap. "It's okay, Tad. You did

279

such a good job. What a good boy. Such a big boy." As I held him, Tad settled back down, then squirmed to get out of my lap and tried to walk again.

A different version of me, one I'd watched earlier, came back on screen. "You're all caught up, Ava. Tad is almost two right now. I'll update this after his second birthday. I'm terribly sorry this has happened again. We grieved hard when a reset made us forget his first birthday. It seems like you and I will be fighting the medicine battle a little longer. I hope we find one that works for us again soon."

The screen went black, and this time, it stayed that way.

Rosie sat at my feet.

"Can I go this time?" I asked her.

She backed out of my way as I stood and stretched. The notebook I'd found after reading my tattoo lay on the bed.

Man, my mother was a piece of work. I hoped I didn't run into her anytime soon. At least I knew where she was and what she looked like.

"What now, Rosie?"

The furry red-gold dog bounded to the doorway, then turned to wait for me.

"I'm coming."

I followed her out of the room into a small hall. On the left was the front door of the house. To the right was the kitchen.

Rosie ran to the back door and used a rope with a ball on the end to open it.

"You want me to go out there?"

Rosie pulled the door open wide. It was a bright, sunshiny afternoon. A sprinkler was going in the yard.

Something flashed past the door in bright yellow.

"Rosie, what was that?"

I stepped forward. Rosie moved ahead of me onto a small concrete porch. She sat down and barked three times.

The bit of yellow appeared again. It was the boy from the video. "Mommy!" He lifted his arms.

Before I could move, he was snatched up by the man from the video. Tucker. My husband.

I took a step back into the doorway.

"Did you get to the end?" he asked.

"I think so. It was Tad's first steps."

"Yes. We should add more videos. We've been meaning to. He can walk quite well now." He hefted the boy onto his hip.

"Mommy, Mommy!" The boy attempted to lunge from Tucker's grasp to get to me.

"Wait a minute, Tad," Tucker said. "Let me talk to Mommy." He turned to me. "This is the first reset where he's old enough to come for you on his own."

Tad squirmed in Tucker's arms. "Mommy, Mommy!"

My belly quivered. "It's okay. Let him come to me."

"You sure?"

"Yes."

He set the boy down. His short legs immediately started pumping, carrying him the last distance to the porch. He was wet, the yellow shirt and shorts soaked from the sprinkler.

I picked him up. "Mommy!" he said, resting his head on my shoulder.

I arranged him on my hip. My body already knew how to hold him. "Yes, Tad," I said. "I'm here."

I didn't know how long it had taken for me to read the

book and watch the videos, but it must have felt like forever to someone so little.

Tucker approached. "You doing okay? Did you take some medicine? You usually have a headache."

I nodded. "Rosie took me to the ibuprofen."

"Good." He clasped his hands behind his back. "I know this is hard."

"I think I'm okay. I don't feel angry or scared like the video said I might." Tad reared back in my arms. "Mommy!"

"Yes, Tad," I said. "Hello."

He squirmed down from my hip. I guessed he was ready to move on.

I set him down, and he took off across the lawn, shrieking as he got sprayed with water.

I sat down on a red metal chair near the door. "He's cute," I said. Watching him play was the most calming thing I'd experienced since I woke up on the bathroom floor.

Tucker sat near my feet. "He is."

I had a thousand questions. Who was I really? Were we in love still, like Ava had said in the video? Did I still take photos? What would happen now that I didn't know anything?

But the sun was warm on my skin. Tucker sat with me quietly, close but without asking anything of me.

And a small boy raced across the glass, forward and back, shouting every time the water turned his way.

Rosie lay on the other side, panting lightly, the words "Seizure Dog" bright and white on the harness on her back.

I reached down to pet her head. We were already acquainted.

And soon, I'd get to know this man beside me. And the boy playing in the grass.

Maybe I didn't know anything yet. But even so, I think I'm going to like it here.

Thank you so much for reading *This Love*. In the Author's Notes, I talk about how epilepsy has affected our family.

For my other emotional reads, I recommend my *USA Today* bestselling book Forever Innocent about how baby loss affects a young couple. Or Forbidden Dance for how a secret adoption is impacted when a birth mother is unexpectedly famous after falling in love with a celebrity.

I find peace in the ups and downs of my life by creating dynamic new situations involving the issues from my own home. They help me cope. I hope they help you, too.

XO, Deanna

The heart remembers.

Author's Note

Seizures were a concern of mine from very early. I had episodes I assumed were just fainting starting in my early teens. I recall careening off my bicycle on hot days, waking up with my face in the grass. I once shouted for my dad right as I went under at the optometrist's office.

To this day, I really don't like doctor visits. I never know when I will faint or seize.

But ultimately, I wasn't diagnosed with epilepsy, but vaso-vagal syncope, which can look very similar.

So, when my daughter had a seizure at age six, I thought, oh no, her, too?

But it was so much worse.

We battled seizures long and hard, with many stays at the children's hospital and med after med after med. She wasn't a candidate for surgery, and many years felt hopeless.

Then, she finished growing. A med combination finally worked. She's in her twenties now, and her life is fine. She drives. She got a culinary degree and works as a pastry chef at a resort. It still feels like a miracle.

Deanna and Elizabeth during their High School Musical movie marathon at Dell Children's epilepsy unit.

I have written several books about epilepsy. My book for nine- to twelve-year-olds is called *Elektra Chaos*, about a girl with epilepsy who saves the world. Elizabeth is actually on the cover.

And, of course, there is *This Kiss*, which is the first part of Ava and Tucker's story from when they meet on the epilepsy unit at age seventeen through their early twenties.

This Love will be followed by one more book, *This Life*. That story will take Ava and Tucker's story through hardship and saving graces, all the way to the last stages of their lives.

Why do I write stories about the things that were difficult in my life? I always have. I've published seven books about baby loss. Several about adoption and foster care. If I've gone through it, I'm going to write about it! Maybe it helps me process those events. Maybe I want to advocate for people in these situations.

But mostly, I want to believe that we can go through hard things and come out the other side. That we can still love and be loved. Live and be happy. That the dark moments might come, but they will pass. Writing stories where this happens is a strategy to cope, and my best way to hold on to hope.

If you're facing hard things, I hope it helps you, too.

Thank you for reading.

Deanna Roy

2025

The heart remembers.

Even more than book one, *This Kiss*, my new book *This Love* is an homage to the city where I've lived most of my life: Austin, Texas.

Most of the places that are important to Ava and Tucker have been important to me, too.

I spent 20 years working as a photographer, including capturing weddings up on Mount Bonnell.

I have climbed the 106 steps up to Mount Bonnell many, many times. Some of my most iconic memories happened up there.

I've led many photography groups through taking images of the best-loved spots in Austin, including Lady Bird Lake and the statue of Stevie Ray Vaughan. I actually met the musician when I worked dressing room security for the now-demolished Frank Erwin Center.

The final scenes of the book, when Ava gives birth to Tad at Seton Central, are taken directly from the hospital where I gave birth to my two biological daughters.

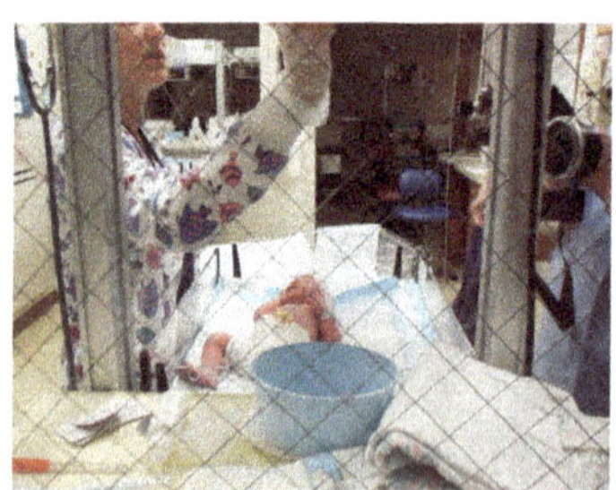

No matter where I end up in this life, Austin has been the place I've called home the longest. It was a delight to talk about this slice of my hometown in a novel.

My other books set in Austin, Texas:

Big Pickle by my JJ Knight pen name

Jinnie Wishmaker (a book for 9-12 year olds)

Deanna Roy is the six-time *USA Today* bestselling author of new adult romance and women's fiction.

She writes passionately from her own life experiences, spinning them into stories. Her books follow the complexity of baby loss (*Baby Dust, Forever Innocent*), adoption and foster care (*Forbidden Dance, Conversations with Little Dude*), and living with epilepsy (*This Kiss, Elektra Chaos.*) She lives in Austin, Texas, with her family.

Learn more about the author at
www.deannaroy.com

Join her email or text list for new release notices at
deannaroy.com/news

facebook.com/deannaroyauthor
instagram.com/deannaroyauthor
bookbub.com/authors/deanna-roy
tiktok.com/@deannaroy.author

THE FOREVER SERIES

A young couple reunites in college, four years after the death of their newborn.

- Forever Innocent (Corabelle & Gavin)
- Forever Loved (Corabelle & Gavin)
- Forever Sheltered (Tina & Darion)
- Forever Bound (Jenny & Chance)
- Forever Family (Corabelle, Tina, Jenny)
- Forever Christmas (Corabelle & Gavin)

- Boxed Set: First Three Books
- Boxed Set: Final Three Books

- Stella and Dane (Standalone)

THIS LOVE SERIES

A woman with a form of epilepsy that causes repeated amnesia resists falling for the man who has pledged to always love her.

- This Kiss
- This Love
- This Life

THE LOVERS DANCE SERIES

A sheltered ballerina is lured into the life of a brash TV reality show star.

- Forbidden Dance
- Wounded Dance
- Wicked Dance
- Tender Dance
- Final Dance

- Lovers Dance Boxed Set

- Billionaire's Dance (a standalone prequel)

OTHER BOOKS

- Conversations with Little Dude (Nonfiction stories with her son who was adopted from foster care)
- In the Company of Angels (A fill-in-the-pages baby record book for babies lost to miscarriage or stillbirth)
- The Magic Mayhem trilogy of action/adventure books for children ages 9-12.

You might also love Deanna's pen name Abby Tyler. As Abby, Deanna writes funny, feel-good small-town romances with a recurring cast of feisty senior citizens and the couples they push together, by hook or by crook.